ALSO BY CHARLES BAXTER

FICTION

Saul and Patsy

The Feast of Love

Believers

Shadow Play

A Relative Stranger

First Light

Through the Safety Net

Harmony of the World

POETRY

Imaginary Paintings

ESSAYS

Beyond Plot

Burning Down the House

THE SOUL THIEF

THE SOUL THIEF

CHARLES BAXTER

PANTHEON BOOKS NEW YORK

Grateful acknowledgment is made to the following for permission to
reprint previously published material:
George Braziller, Inc.: Excerpt from "Golden State" from *Golden State*
by Frank Bidart (New York: George Braziller, Inc., 1973).
Reprinted by permission of George Braziller, Inc.
Oxford University Press: Excerpt from "The Census-Takers"
from *Selected Poems* by Conrad Aiken (Oxford: Oxford
University Press, 2003). Reprinted by permission
of Oxford University Press.

Library of Congress Cataloging-in-Publication Data

Baxter, Charles, [date]
The soul thief / Charles Baxter.
p. cm.
ISBN 978-0-375-42252-2
1. Graduate students—Fiction. 2. Buffalo (N.Y.)—Fiction.
I. Title.
PS3552.A854S68 2007
813'.54—dc22
2007018119

www.pantheonbooks.com
Printed in the United States of America
First Edition
2 4 6 8 9 7 5 3 1

For Michael Scrivener and Mary Ann Simmons
and for Ross Pudaloff

I dreamed I *had* my wish:

      — I seemed to see
the conditions of my life, upon
a luminous stage: how I could change,
how I could not: the root of necessity,
and choice.

—FRANK BIDART, "GOLDEN STATE"

PART ONE

1

HE WAS INSUFFERABLE, one of those boy geniuses, all nerve and brain.

Before I encountered him in person, I heard the stories. They told me he was aberrant ("abnormal" is too plain an adjective to apply to him), a whiz-kid sage with a wide range of affectations. He was given to public performative thinking. When his college friends lounged in the rathskeller, drinking coffee and debating Nietzsche, he sipped tea through a sugar cube and undermined their arguments with quotations from Fichte. The quotations were not to be found, however, in the volumes where he said they were. They were not anywhere.

He performed intellectual surgery using hairsplitting distinctions. At the age of nineteen, during spring break, he took up strolling through Prospect Park with a walking stick and a fedora. Even the pigeons stared at him. Not for him the beaches in Florida, or nudity in its physical form, or the vulgarity of joy. He did not often change clothes, preferring to wear the same shirt until it had become ostentatiously threadbare. He carried around the old-fashioned odor of bohemia. He was homely. His teachers feared him. Sometimes, while thinking, he appeared to daven like an Orthodox Jew.

He was an adept in both classical and popular cultures. For example, he had argued that after the shower scene in Hitchcock's *Psycho,* Marion Crane isn't dead, but she isn't not-dead either, because the iris in her eyeball is constricted in that gigantic close-up matching the close-up of the shower drain. The irises of the dead are dilated. Hers are not. So, in some sense, she's still alive, though the blood is pouring out of her wounds.

When Norman Bates carries Marion Crane's body, wrapped in a shower curtain, to deposit in the trunk of her car for disposal, they cross the threshold together like a newly married couple, but in a backwards form, in reverse, a psychotic transvestite (as cross-dressers were then called) and a murdered woman leaving the room, having consummated something. The boy genius wouldn't stop to explain what a backwards-form marriage might consist of with such a couple, what its shared mortal occasion might have been. With him, you had to consider such categories carefully and conjure them up for yourself, alone, later, lying in bed, sleepless.

Here I have to perform a tricky maneuver, because I am implicated in everything that happened. The maneuver's logic may become clear before my story is over. I must turn myself into a "he" and give myself a bland Anglo-Saxon Protestant name. Any one of them will do as long as the name recedes into a kind of anonymity. The surname that I will therefore give myself is "Mason." An equally inconspicuous given name is also required. Here it is: "Nathaniel." So that is who I am: Nathaniel Mason. He once said that the name "Nathaniel" was cursed, as "Ahab" and "Judas" and

"Lee Harvey" were cursed, and that my imagination had been poisoned at its source by what people called me. "Or else it could be, you know, that your imagination heaves about like a broken algorithm," he said, "and *that* wouldn't be so bad, if you could find another algorithm at the horizon of your, um, limitations."

He himself was Jerome Coolberg. A preposterous moniker, nonfictional, uninvented by him, an old man's name, someone who totters through Prospect Park stabilized with a cane. No one ever called him "Jerry." It was always "Jerome" or "Coolberg." He insisted on both for visibility and because as names they were as dowdy as a soiled woolen overcoat. Still, like the coat, the name seemed borrowed from somewhere. All his appearances had an illusionary but powerful electrical charge. But the electricity was static electricity and went nowhere, though it could maim and injure. By "illusionary" I mean to say that he was a thief. And what he tried to do was to steal souls, including mine. He appeared to have no identity of his own. From this wound, he bled to death, like Marion Crane, although for him death was not fatal.

2

ON A COOL autumn night in Buffalo, New York, the rain has diminished to a mere streetlight-hallucinating drizzle, and Nathaniel Mason has taken off his sandals and carries them in one hand, the other hand holding a six-pack of Iroquois Beer sheltered against his stomach like a marsupial's pouch. He advances across an anonymous park toward a party whose address was given to him over the phone an hour ago by genially drunk would-be scholars. On Richmond? Somewhere near Richmond. Or Chenango. These young people his own age, graduate students like himself, have gathered to drink and to socialize in one of this neighborhood's gigantic old houses now subdivided into apartments. It is the early 1970s, days of ecstatic bitterness and joyfully articulated rage, along with fear, which is unarticulated. *Life Against Death* stands upright on every bookshelf.

The spokes of the impossibly laid-out streets defy logic. Maps are no help. Nathaniel is lost, being new to the baroque brokenness of this city. He holds the address of the apartment on a sopping piece of paper in his right hand, the hand that is also holding the beer, as he tries to read the directions and the street names. The building (or house—he doesn't know which it is) he searches for is somewhere near Kleinhans Music Hall—north or south, the directions being contradictory. His long hair falls over his eyes as he peers down at the nonsensical address.

The city, as a local wit has said, gives off the phosphorescence of decay. Buffalo runs on spare parts. Zoning is a joke; residential housing finds itself next to machine shops and factories for windshield wipers, and, given even the mildest wind, the mephitic air smells of burnt wiring and sweat. Rubbish piles up in plain view. What is apparent everywhere here is the noble shabbiness of industrial decline. The old apartment buildings huddle against one another, their bricks collapsing together companionably. Nathaniel, walking barefoot through the tiny park as he clutches his beer, his sandals, and the address, imagines a city of this sort abandoned by the common folk and taken over by radicals and students and intellectuals like himself—Melvillians, Hawthornians, Shakespeareans, young Hegelians—all of whom understand the mysteries and metaphors of finality, the poetry of lastness, ultimaticity—the architecture here is unusually *fin de* something, though not *siècle,* certainly not that—who are capable, these youths, of turning ruination inside out. Their young minds, subtly productive, might convert anything, including this city, into brilliance. The poison turns as if by magic into the antidote. From the resources of imagination, decline, and night, they will build a new economy, these youths, never before seen.

The criminal naïveté of these ideas amuses him. Why not be criminally naïve? Ambition *requires* hubris. So does idealism. Why not live in a state of historical contradiction? What possible harm can there be in such intellectual narcissism, in the Faustian overreaching of radical reform?

Even the upstate New York place-names seem designed for transformative pathos and comedy: "Parkside" where there is no real park, streets and cemeteries in honor of the thirteenth president, Millard Fillmore, best known for having introduced the flush toilet into the White House, and . . . ah, here is a young woman, dressed as he himself is, in jeans and t-shirt, though she is also wearing an Army surplus flak jacket, which fits her rather well and is accessorized with Soviet medals probably picked up from a European student black market. Near the curb, she holds her hand to her forehead as she checks the street addresses. She is, fortunately, also lost, and gorgeous in an intellectual manner, with delicate features and piercing eyes. Her brown hair is held back in a sort of Ph.D. ponytail.

They introduce themselves. They are both graduate students, both looking for the same mal-addressed party, a party in hiding. In homage to his gesture, she takes off her footwear and puts her arm in his. This is the epoch of bare feet in public life; it is also the epoch of instantaneous bondings. Nathaniel quickly reminds her—her name is Theresa, which she pronounces *Teraysa,* as if she were French, or otherwise foreign—that they have met before here in Buffalo, at a political meeting whose agenda had to do with resistance to the draft and the war. But with her flashing eyes, she has no interest in his drabby small talk, and she playfully mocks his Midwestern accent, particularly the nasalized vowels. This is an odd strategy, because her Midwestern accent is as broad and flat as his own. She presents herself with enthusiasm; she has made her banality exotic. She has met everyone; she knows everyone. Her anarchy is perfectly balanced with her hyperacuity about tone and timbre and atmosphere and drift. With her, the time of day is either high noon or midnight. But right now, she simply wants to find the locale of this damn party.

Again the rain starts.

Nathaniel and Theresa pass a park bench. "Let's sit down here for a sec," she says, pointing. She grins. Maybe she doesn't want to find the party after all. "Let's sit down in the rain. We'll get soaked. You'll be the Yin and I'll be . . . the other one. The Yang." She points her index finger at him, assigning him a role.

"What? Why?" Nathaniel has no idea what she is talking about.

"*Why?* Because it's so Gene Kelly, that's why. Because it's not done. No *sensible* person sits down in the rain." She salts the word "sensible" with cheerful derision. "It's not, I don't know, *wise.* There's the possibility of viral pneumonia, right? You'd have to be a character in a Hollywood musical to sit down in the rain. Anyway, we'll arrive at the party soaking wet. Our clothes will be attached to our skin, and we'll be *visible.*" She seems to inflect all her adjectives unnecessarily. Also, she has a habit of laughing subvocally after every other sentence, as if she were monitoring her own conversation and found herself wickedly amusing. Together they do as she suggests, and she takes his hand in a moment of what seems to be spontaneous fellow feeling. "I can stand a little rain," she says quietly, fingering his fingers, quoting from somewhere. She leans back on the park bench to let the droplets fall into her eyes. To see her is heaven, Nathaniel thinks. No wonder she wears a flak jacket. They wait there. A minute passes. "Boompadoop-boom ba da boompadoopboom," she sings, Comden-and-Greenishly.

"Look at that," he says, pointing to a building opposite them. Through the second-floor window of a huge run-down house, the party that they have been seeking is visible. The nondifferentiated uproar of conversation floods out onto the street and makes its way to them in the drizzle. To his left, he sees a bum standing under a diseased elm, eyeing them. "That's it. That's us. There's the party. We found it."

Theresa straightens, squints, wiping water from her eyes. "Yes. You're right. There's the place. What a wreck. I hope it has a fire escape. Hey, I think I see that kid, Coolberg," she says. "Right there. Near the second window. On the right. See him?"

"Who?"

"Coolberg? Oh, he's a . . . something. Nobody knows what he is, actually. He hangs out. He has some grand destiny, he says, which he's trying to discover. On Tuesday last week he was going around saying that *art is the pond scum on the stream of commerce,* but on Thursday he was saying that *art is not superstructural but constitutes the base.* Well, he'd better decide which it is. He changes his mind a lot. He's a genius but very queer."

"Queer how?"

"Well, in the *good* way," Theresa says. She thoughtlessly puts her hand on his thigh and strokes it. "Maybe he'll tell you how he's being blackmailed. That's one of his best stories. Come on," she says.

After standing up, she twirls around a lamppost and then dances barefoot into the street, neatly avoiding a car before managing a splashing two-step into a puddle, holding out her sandals as props, a serious Marxist hoofer, this girl, and Nathaniel, who can't match her steps with his own, is stricken, as who would not be, by love-lightning for her. He follows her. The bum stays outside under the elm, watching them go.

In the apartment doorway everyone gets it. "You're soaked! That is so cool. This is very MGM, you two. Did you just kiss out there? Standing up or sitting down? Do you even *know* each other? Did you just meet? Are you guys in a Stanley Donen movie or a Vincente Minnelli movie? Have you been introduced? Do you need to be? Do you want to dry off or is that soaked look a thing that you'd like to keep going for a while? Want a joint, want a beer? The beer's in the kitchen and there's more out on the fire escape unless someone stole it or squirreled it away. Why not sit down right here, on this floor? There's whiskey if you want it. Is Marcuse correct about repressive tolerance or is 'repressive tolerance' another example of the collapse of that particular and once viable Frankfurt Institut für Sozialforschung nonsense? Buying off the masses with material goods? Well, everyone knows the answer to *that* question. Don't stand out there. Come in. Dry off. Join the party."

They do come in, they do attempt to dry off with kitchen rags, they drop their sandals in a pile of sneakers and boots and sandals by the door. Almost immediately, while Nathaniel is recalibrating his emotions in relation to the woman he has just partnered across the street, she disappears into another room. Holding a beer bottle (he has misplaced the six-pack that he himself had brought—perhaps it is still out on the bench in the park and is now being consumed by the elm-bum), he damply threads his way through the corridors of the party, long dreamlike hallways of grouped couples, trios, and quartets. His clothes stick to his skin. The smell of dope and cigarette smoke, the pollution produced by thought, mingles with the aroma of whatever is cooking in the tiny kitchen, where a whitish semi-liquid chive dip has been laid out on a gouged table, bread crusts of some sort piled on a plate nearby, and after he leans over for a bite of whatever it is, Nathaniel stops, pauses, before a disembodied conversation about Joseph Conrad's Eastern gaze on Western eyes—the novelist is treated with friendly condescension for writing a variety of Polish in English that mistakes particularity for substance—a conversation that transitions into the weekend's football game and the prospects of the Buffalo Bills. Someone in another room is singing "Which Side Are You On?" in a good tenor voice. Soon, having wandered in front of a phonograph, he hears, first, Joe Cocker, and quickly after that, Edith Piaf, the turntable being of the old-fashioned type with a spindle and a stack of LPs slapping down, one after the other, a vinyl collage, "*Non, je ne regrette rien*," followed several minutes later by the Mahavishnu Orchestra, out of tune as usual, playing "Open Country Joy."

The party carries with it a mood of heady desperation held in check by the usual energies of youth. When Nathaniel looks at his friends, they remind him of puppies in a cardboard box. What is Nixon, what is Vietnam, what is double-digit inflation and mounting unemployment and a life with no prospects compared to a woman sitting on a broken sofa with a guy whose beard hair is still unassertively spawning, the two of them arguing about *The Eighteenth Brumaire of Louis Bonaparte*? Can the middle class fall outside of history, and, if it does, will actors take over public roles? Sure they will. They already have.

Nathaniel moves away from this group and finds himself in the hallway, where a student composer in the music school—he has been identified as somebody's boyfriend—is describing his latest composition, an overture for strings, clarinets, and percussion entitled *Holiday in Israel*.

"Yeah," the composer says to the ceiling, "klezmer music interrupted by glissando runs on the strings for the missiles and bass drum hits for the explosions."

Nathaniel nods semi-affably. Although he lived for several years in Manhattan, his origins are in Milwaukee, and he has never known a composer before, although he has been forced to listen to highbrow music all his life. The composer says that he hasn't actually written the music down and has yet to decide whether he'll bother. Like concept art, his compositions are still hypothesis music, and *concepts may be more interesting, more varied, and more challenging than the actualities they give rise to.* "For example, you take Leverkühn's music," he says, inhaling so deeply from his unfiltered Egyptian oval that his voice is changed to swamp-speech. "Leverkühn's music," the composer claims, gasping with arrogance, "which is unwritten, is considerably better than Schönberg's, which happens to exist." Who is Leverkühn? Nathaniel shrugs inwardly. The composer announces that he may be forced to stage a première of his work at a nonsense-concert, a noncert, in the Buffalo Noncert Series. All of the noncerts on campus are unannounced and, in effect, unscheduled; instead, they are rumored, until the rumors force them to happen. Noncerts, according to their own motto, "happen to happen."

Annoyed, Nathaniel wanders down the hallway, enveloped by his would-be confidants. Hysterical intellectualism is the norm at parties like this one. The Vietnam War has forced everyone to take up an ideology, to seek a conversion. Everyone needs to be saved, right now, instantly saved from history itself, the factuality of it.

Where is his beer? He has misplaced it. Someone hands him a bottle of vodka. He takes a swig, and the ice-cold iridescent fire leaps in two directions, downward into his stomach and upward into his brain. *A bad idea,* he realizes, with italics, first to drink beer and then vodka. He hands back the vodka bottle to an anonymous and genderless recipient. *Thank you.* The floor's wood feels pleasantly gritty, almost reassuring, on the soles of his bare wet feet, though this floor swells a bit like the ocean, and then the party's hysteria and gloom and desperation suddenly overtake him, while simultaneously a flickering lightbulb in a table lamp separates into two lightbulbs, and Nathaniel realizes that he has ingested a bit too much of the vodka bottle's contents in those two mouthfuls. He is quite instantaneously bleary and vague and half sick. A large head appears before him in the hallway, supported by a body too small for it, the body and the head belonging to Bob Rimjsky, always recognizable because in this crowd of daily informality expressed in jeans and tatters, Rimjsky invariably wears a three-piece suit with a watch chain, another irony, though of what kind—political or personal or horological—it is impossible to guess. On his delicate small feet are tasseled loafers. Not for him the shedding of footwear out in the foyer. For him, the revolution will take the form of ubiquitous formality. Something about him resembles the owl. Like almost all the men here, he has a beard, though unlike the others, his baritone voice is monotonously fixed to one tone, creating a comic drone effect, a vaudeville owl, or a bored investment counselor among the unwashed, playing his 33 rpm statements at 16 rpm. Unlike the beautiful Theresa, Rimjsky never emphasizes a single word in his sentences, and the mad stare common to this time and place that Rimjsky uses when he begins speaking simply adds to his steadfast personal monotony.

"You're wet," he observes in a scholarly manner. "Is that deliberate?"

Nathaniel nods before looking down the hallway.

"Don't go in there, Mason." Rimjsky nods toward another room, a bedroom. "I wouldn't go in there if I were you."

"Why?" Nathaniel asks. The door to the bedroom stands half open.

"Coolberg's in there. He's talking about his dreams. Stay away from that."

"So what's the matter with dreams?"

"Everything. Don't you know Coolberg?" The noise of the party seems to reach a crescendo before dying away. Nathaniel feels a fingernail on his back. Theresa has passed by and has touched him. "I thought everyone knew him."

"No. I've just heard of him. You're the second person tonight who's mentioned the guy." Nathaniel is about to excuse himself to pursue Theresa when Rimjsky grabs his arm in a laconic gesture.

"Coolberg's always striking one pose or another. But listen, Mason, he's dangerous. And that's an adjective I have never in my life used until now. You'll think at first that he has no known location, but he's as real as we are," Rimjsky drones, conversation-as-hypnosis, a monotonality that makes Nathaniel sleepy. "He's the first person I've known who can be in two places at once. He's dislocated. Not a joint or a knee—the whole person."

Rimjsky scratches his beard to prevent interruption or response.

"Of course he's brilliant. He's a virtuoso of cast-off ideas," he continues. "And he may be a genius. I don't care. Genius doesn't impress me. You'll notice that he doesn't assert ownership over his ideas. He's in some kind of Artaudian condition where all the ideas are unoriginated and unsourced; that's how he can claim anybody else's ideas as his own. Really all he wants to do is acquire everyone's inner life. I'd use the word 'soul,' but I don't believe in souls. Still, it's like a Russian novel, what he does. He inhabits a dense spiritual vacuum. I apologize for the phrase, but that's what it is. Don't go in there."

When Nathaniel glances again inside the room, he sees, through the crack of the door opening, Theresa sitting on the floor. She's attentively watching someone out of Nathaniel's view. "Aw, come on. Don't be melodramatic," Nathaniel says to Rimjsky, whose eyes, he now notices, do not ever blink, although they are wide and predatory. Glancing down at the floor, he urges the door to the left with his knee, but before entering the room, he pauses to listen to the voice emanating from it.

The tone of the voice he hears is calmly agitated, as if it had lived with its own agitation for so long that it had grown slightly bored with the ongoing crisis of its condition, a crisis so complex and multilayered that no effort could possibly repair it or even define the nature of its own apparent suffering. The voice has a pleading note, halfway between seduction and distress, and an intelligent gentleness that is all the more alarming for its measured calm, its burnt-over benumbed despair. It sounds, Nathaniel realizes, like a therapist's voice, thick with overeager compassion, but it also seems at almost any moment about to modulate into mad spattering giggles. The voice performs code-switching out of apparent sincerity into malevolent amusement and then into excited despair.

The voice, it seems, *is* reporting a recent dream.

"I was in a gigantic white lavish hotel that was on fire, done for," the voice behind the door claims with comic mournfulness, "but the fire was consuming the hotel so gradually and deliberately that people were still permitted to arrive and depart freely. The fire wasn't visible, but I knew the hotel was burning because smoke was hanging thinly everywhere, especially around the lights. Very beautiful, that smoke. I returned to my room to save my valuables, and I couldn't find them, whatever they were. I didn't know what to search for, what I had to save, how soon the building would collapse, what I had to do. Everyone was busy and wandering around but it was quiet and a little slowed." The voice pauses. "The elevators were golden. There were cupids carved into the ceiling. I was strangely alone although people were all around. They kept disappearing. No one told me what to do, but I worried because, after all, I was neglecting them or not doing something I was supposed to do. It was like an emergency in slow motion."

"That's not your dream!" Theresa tells him. "That's someone else's dream. You took it."

"Why do you say that?" Coolberg asks. "Why do you say that it's not mine?"

"Because . . . you *can't* have a dream like that," she informs him. "Men don't have burning-hotel dreams. That's a woman's dream." Coolberg starts laughing as if caught out, and Nathaniel chooses at this moment to enter the room, just as Coolberg is saying, "Well, all right, then tell me what dreams a man is supposed to have."

In the room five people glance at Nathaniel, their expressions ranging from indifference to curiosity. Two people whisper to each other near the bookcase, and, closer to the doorway, Theresa and Coolberg and an albino dwarfish man sit together on the floor by the bed. They share a beer, the bottle moving around from hand to hand. The albino gets up to leave. A certain intimacy at once falls between Coolberg and Theresa; they have the appearance of unindicted

co-conspirators who share a complicated system of signals—
lifted eyebrows, glances, finger flicks—all seemingly worked
out in advance. Coolberg glances at Nathaniel, and Theresa
says, "Well, look who's here. It's Nathaniel. My soaked twin."

"Hello," Coolberg says. "Oh, yes. You're Nathaniel Mason.
I've heard a lot about you. But they're perfunctory things.
Sit down." Theresa pats the floor next to her. Nathaniel
notices a small puddle of water under her jeans. From the
rain. Soon a small puddle of water will form under himself,
as he drains onto the floor.

Nathaniel gamely lowers himself to their level. Coolberg
smiles at him menacingly. Years later he will realize that
Coolberg's first words to him consisted of a false claim, followed by a command, a pattern for their friendship, and that
this charade was acted out in front of Theresa, who, like an
accommodating audience member, encouraged the show.
Once again, and equally thoughtlessly, she puts her hand on
his—Nathaniel's—leg. Coolberg sees her do it. "Nathaniel,
you're so *cute* when you're wet," she says. "You're flagrant."

"What is this, the state fair?" Coolberg asks.

Nathaniel takes in Coolberg's face, stricken by a kind of
internalized warfare. In one moment he appears to be a
sickly child in a room through whose one window a winter
sun shines in, briefly, at twilight, giving the child the farewell
gift of its fading rusty light on the snow; in the next moment
the expression diagnoses itself, disintegrates, and recom-
bines into one of all-encompassing sympathy, before it turns
bewilderingly into an Asia-Minorish sedulous gaze from
one of the booths at the bazaar. The eyes miss nothing, but
they are spectacularly dead.

"I don't know anything about you," Nathaniel says.
"Except what people tell me."

"Oh, what do they tell you?" Coolberg asks, delightedly, mockingly, dolorously, sweetly.

"See, that would be telling. What do you do, when you're doing things?"

"You're quoting *The Prisoner*. 'That would be telling.' As for me, I do everything," Coolberg says, clumsily lighting up a Lucky.

"Guys, guys!" Theresa interrupts, very pleased to pretend that the two men are engaged in combat rather than verbal trickery, as she looks around the bedroom for an ashtray.

"I do everything," Coolberg repeats. And then he starts singing.

> *"I've made a path*
> *as a polymath*
> *that no one else has trod!"*

Theresa perks up. "*He's made a path as a polymath that no one else has trod!*" She gives a whoop of laughter. "Siggie, you're so Broadway."

Who is Siggie? Coolberg ashes his cigarette into a beer bottle. These are juvenile tiresome antics; the anxious high spirits have a depressing effect. *To hell with these people,* the vodka says to Nathaniel, whereupon he stands up. He feels a bit unsteady, like a bird on a branch whipped by winds. Being upright is a continuous struggle. There must be others at this party to whom he can talk about something, or nothing. He experiences wanly the need for quiet and sincerity, some antidote to cleverness. He could go back to wherever he parked his car, drive home to his empty apartment, and then read until sleep takes him over just before dawn. In all-out verbal gamesmanship, he will be seriously overmatched here. He can't keep up with these people. Half the time, he regards himself as a hayseed among city slickers. A sudden heavy hayseed loneliness envelops him, as it often does at parties, like the onset of an illness. His limbs feel weighted down, and objects take on the burden of hopelessness. The other faces at the party look as if they had been painted on the sides of balloons, and from the books on the floor he thinks he hears an angry buzzing like the sound of insects.

"What's the matter? Don't you like it?" Coolberg asks.

"No," Nathaniel says, having forgotten what the "it" refers to. Then he remembers. "Oh, it's all right. By the way, who's Siggie?"

"Sigmund Romberg. The composer of *Blossom Time*."

Theresa reaches for Nathaniel's hand. "Don't leave," she says. "Sit? Please? Here, beside me?"

Perhaps she likes him. Maybe she'll heal him of his solitude. And then, as if he had been reading Nathaniel's mind, Coolberg says, "You know, there's something heartsick about parties like this. Look at us. We're all pretending to be smart, as if intelligence were the cure for our anguish. We're all making this verbal clatter. We cluck our thick tongues . . . and speak oh so very politely. Aren't you cold? Your clothes are soaked. Theresa's, too. Did you take a shower together? Fully clothed? Why would anyone *do* that?"

"Oh, I'll survive."

"That wasn't my question."

What was his question? Nathaniel can't remember it. He sits down again and leans his damp self against Theresa. She is as warm as a radiator filling with steam.

3

Two or more hours later (Nathaniel does not wear a watch on principle—he refuses to be a slave to any clock), still damp, and now thoroughly bleary with alcohol, behind the wheel of his rusting dark-butterscotch-colored VW Beetle, Nathaniel maneuvers around the streets of Buffalo in an effort to take Coolberg back to his apartment and Theresa back to hers. When Theresa asks him whether he's drunk and thus unfit to drive, Nathaniel shouts proudly, "I've been driving drunk since the age of sixteen." He must shout. No intimate conversation has ever been carried on in a VW Beetle; the motor's chain drive creates too much commotion for reflective conversation. Talking in such a car is like orating into the surf.

At a street corner, as they stop at a red light, Nathaniel sees a woman standing and staring at him mutely. No doubt the look she is giving him has nothing behind it, no intention beyond curiosity. And yet he feels accused. These people follow him around.

The implementation of the favor that he is performing has grown complicated: Coolberg lives farther away from

Nathaniel's apartment than Theresa does, but it is essential that the boy genius be disposed of quickly in case Theresa wants to prolong the evening. Meanwhile, Coolberg has taken up the subject of solitude again, quite loudly. "You know what I think? I think we're all in our private traps, clamped in them. We scratch and claw, but only at the air, only at each other, and for all of it, we never budge an inch."

Theresa suddenly barks a command from the tiny backseat. "Stop making speeches," she shouts over the noise of the engine. "Stop quoting. You don't believe that! That's not you."

Coolberg laughs. "Nothing is me." He looks over at Nathaniel with a boyish expectancy. "Nathaniel, I liked what you said about polio and iron lungs." Nathaniel tries to remember what he has said about that subject. He doesn't recall having any opinions about polio. "Let's talk again. Let's go to Niagara Falls or something. Have you ever been to the falls at night? The gods come out there in the dark. Really, they do. Or we could go to the Mirrored Room." The Mirrored Room, by Lucas Samaras, is a well-known fixture of the local art museum. In this room, the floor, ceiling, and walls are made of mirrors; the body dissolves there. "You can let me out right now," he says unexpectedly. "This is my place. I'll call you."

The building outside of which they have stopped is yet another Buffalo structure, a large upstate New York house on a tiny lot, the front lawn so small that it could be mowed in two minutes. Nothing separates this house from the one next to it except a driveway. The neighborhood is cluttered and congested with houses; in this jungle of domiciles, trees have been forced out, to live elsewhere. Coolberg scrambles out of the car and walks in a slouching ramble toward the front door. Nathaniel would like to see him enter the house—he is not completely sure that Coolberg actually resides here—but in the meantime, Theresa has clambered into the front seat and has closed the door.

"Onward and upward," she says, smiling briskly, as she loosens the rubber band from her ponytail so that her hair drops onto her shoulders. She puts the rubber band in her mouth and chews it as she fluffs out her hair. Suddenly she looks very naked.

Nathaniel drives to the end of the block. "Where to?" he asks. "Want to come back to my place?" With some effort, he creates a likely scenario. "We could talk. I could make scrambled eggs and coffee, and we could watch the sun come up."

Theresa smiles, amused by him. "No, not tonight." She touches the back of his neck in a seemingly tender gesture, though it feels more like a tease than affection. "I'm too gone. I'm much too gone to have breakfast with you."

"We don't have to do anything," he says, not wanting to sound desperate. "We don't have to have a meal together."

"Take a right here," she tells him, pointing at a streetlight up ahead. He signals a turn and follows her next instructions for another minute or so. Someone half a block away shouts or screams. City sounds.

"I want to call you. I want to see you again. Is that okay?"

"I guess so." She sighs. "Just not tonight. We should be . . . I don't know, *alert.* If I ever sleep with you, I want to be stone-cold sober. Besides, I already have somebody." She takes out a slip of paper from her damp flak jacket and writes down her phone number. "Even though he's not important and can be disposed of, I've got him. He's not here, but he *is* somewhere. He exists, I mean. He has a residence. Anyway, I haven't thought through the whole monogamy thing"—she shouts over the noise of the motor—

"so I don't have a position on sleeping with you. Yet." She puts the slip of paper into his shirt's front pocket. "Do you have somebody? You're so cute you should never be alone." In the noise created by the VW's acceleration, the question seems loud and rhetorical, unanswerable, and a bit mean-spirited, coming from this beautiful woman who twice (or was it three times?) placed her hand on Nathaniel's thigh. Does Theresa enjoy creating desire in him just to see herself doing it? To establish that she herself is unmoved? Like a laboratory scientist? Or a sleepy cat with its prey? That she can cast spells, that she is powerful? A rash of questions.

He therefore does not answer her inquiry about whether he has someone because the answer is "No, not now," and those words are not the ones he wishes to utter as he shifts into second gear, sober from the intensity of loneliness and arousal and late-night animal longing. His hands are sweaty and he can't think straight, and he feels sick with alcoholic lust, damp clothes, desolation, and maybe even neon-lighted love. Right now he would sleep with anything beautiful, if only beauty would sleep with him, this beauty or any other.

"Up there," she says. "I'm up there." They have found themselves on Hertel, and she points to an ice-cream shop, Lickety Split. Her apartment, she claims, is located upstairs from the ice cream and the service people who scoop it and the customers who eat it. All day, Nathaniel imagines, she inhales the smell of waffle cones. That's what he smelled on her earlier: confectionary scents, cream and sugar spackled all over this girl.

"Good night," whispers Theresa, giving him a peck on the cheek. Then she touches his face under the cheekbone with her finger, a kind of mini-caress. It feels like a depth charge, coming from her. "I've wanted to touch you in that spot all night," she confesses. *This is unlawful,* Nathaniel thinks, *the carnival style, the show-biz way she touches me.* He reaches over to lay a hand on her, but she has maneuvered out of reach. "Give me a call . . . or something."

She glances down as she shuts the car door, and Nathaniel can see her grinning to herself privately, as if she liked him once upon a time, hours ago; but for him to return that smile through the car window, the minimal effort invested in *any* facial expression, hardly seems worth the trouble. It would require optimism and a heroic spirit. He would have to hire a crane to lift his mouth into a grin. The entire evening has turned into a dead battery. It doesn't matter what you hook it up to. Nothing will go anywhere because no motor will start.

In the light of the car's high beams, he watches Theresa, accessorized with her flak jacket and her shiny tin medals of Lenin, her homage to the material world, skip up the side-walk to her building, enter the front door to the foyer, efficiently take out a key, and make her beauty-pageant progress inside. A horrible thought: She is not drunk or tired at all. She's just had enough of him.

4

WHAT WOULD GERTRUDE STEIN say about this
evening?

*For a long time being one being living he had been trying to be certain
that he had known what he was doing standing and sitting where it was
raining, and when he had come to be certain that he did not know and could
not know that he was doing what he was doing with another who was also
magnificent and living, that was the time he was certain that he would be
driving to where he was concluding this evening and other evenings, and he
certainly was driving, and anyway everyone agreed that he was driving to
where he alone was concluding and sleeping.* Occasionally Gertrude
Stein explains his life to him, for the relief. She has accompanied him at odd moments ever since he heard her
recorded voice one afternoon on the car radio as he was
driving around doing errands.

When Nathaniel reaches his own apartment, half of a
duplex on a seedy cul-de-sac near the campus, the front
door has been jimmied open, and, for some reason, his mail-
box has been unlocked to reveal its lack of contents. He
steps inside and observes in the half-dark that the lamp near
the entryway is now turned over and is lying sideways on the

floor, a burglary prop. Somebody with a flashlight is fossick-
ing in Nathaniel's bedroom, pulling the drawers open, emp-
tying them, checking the closets.

"Hey, you," Nathaniel calls out. "What're you doing?
What in the fucking hell is this?"

The flashlight shines in his direction. "Me?" The voice is
slurred. "Who're you, man?" Nathaniel, who has been around
the druggy block a few times, recognizes it as junkie speech.
The tone carries with it an aura of super-sedated vagueness,
along with a fuzzy pointless aggression, and the voice res-
onates with that sleepy absentminded hipster attitude.

"Who am I? I *live* here," Nathaniel says to the burglar.
"Fuck you. This is my place."

"Well, this *place* is pathetic," the burglar mutters. "You got
nothin' to steal. Less than nothing. This stuff is all complete
shit. This is what you return to the store the day after
Christmas. It's like a church basement in here. I'm wasting
my valuable time."

"I know," Nathaniel says, sitting down. He leans his head
back against the wall, feeling a kind of Buddhist indifference
to everything.

"All you got is these fucking paperbacks. Books every
damn where. A lamp that doesn't work. This junk clock
radio. And a fuckin' coffeepot," the flashlight says directly
into his face. "Which is *rusting*. A rusting coffeepot! How
come you live this way? I got it better than you. And your
clothes are all wet. What's that?"

"I'm just a graduate student."

"You don't even have a *bike*. Or a stereo."

"So?" Nathaniel says, feeling too tired to challenge him. "I
walk everywhere or take the bus," he lies. The VW, after
all, had been a grudging gift from his stepfather, and the
burglar might want to steal it. But, no; once having seen its

butterscotch-colored paint job, no thief would want it. Nathaniel waits. "You going to leave now? There's nothing here for you."

The burglar sighs. "Don't I know it. You're not going to attack me or nothin'?" he asks. He is young also, probably Nathaniel's age, stoned, but—Nathaniel can see this in the semi-dark—wearing a wedding ring.

"No," Nathaniel says. "Why would I do that?"

"Well," the voice asks, coming out of the flashlight, "would you make me a cup of coffee, then? I don't care if it tastes of rust. This has been an awful night." Nathaniel reaches for the light switch, and the burglar says, "No, don' do that. I can't have you seein' me."

"Oh, okay," Nathaniel says. So all right. So why not make a cup of coffee for a burglar? It is a revolutionary act. After going into the kitchen, he fills his coffeepot, the Mighty Midget, with Breakfast Blend and water, lets the brew percolate, and pours a cup. "Cream or sugar?" he calls out.

The burglar has nodded off on the sofa. "Cream or sugar?" Nathaniel repeats more loudly, approaching the guy, who smells of anise. Nathaniel shakes the burglar's shoulder. The intruder still has a flashlight in one hand, a toy gun in the other, and a grocery bag at his feet.

"Aaargh," the guy says. "No. I hate sugar. Sugar is a disguise. It's bad for you. Gives me headaches. Black, just black, okay?"

"Okay, sure," Nathaniel says. After returning to the kitchen, he pours the intruder and himself each a cup of coffee, goes back to the sofa, hands one of them to the guy, and sits down on the other side of the room from him.

"So," Nathaniel says to the young man, in the near-dark, "you're married?"

"Yuh," the man says. "And my old lady got a baby on the way." He sips the coffee. "Soon, too. See, I lost my job months ago. I was a janitor. Welfare's run out and shit. She can't work, my wife. She broke her leg in a fall she took downtown. Marble stairs, slippery, you know? Maybe we could sue. She just gimps around. Like a *bug*. What it is, we don't have no parents, the two of us, like most people do."

"Too bad." Nathaniel waits. "Of course it doesn't help things that you've got a habit. You must be a crummy thief if you shoot up before you go out to steal things."

The man doesn't respond to the critique of his lifestyle. "How come you live like this, man?" the burglar asks, sipping at his hot coffee, his voice calm. "This is one motherfuckin' friendless apartment." He pauses, contemplating it. "Are you a Spartan or something? 'Cause a lonesome soul lives here, I'll tell you that. I wouldn't be able to stand it. Shit. I'd get me a comfortable chair, at least. And a TV set. Don't you watch TV? Football? Johnny Carson?"

Nathaniel shakes his head. And, before dawn breaks, he tells the burglar about the entire night, about himself, his studies, his former home in Milwaukee, and how Theresa would not come home with him, which, considering the burglar's presence, was probably a happy accident.

"You're okay, man," the burglar says a few minutes later, before he shakes Nathaniel's hand to leave. "But, you know, you should get better locks on your door. You know, the dead-bolt kind? The kind you got here, they won't stop a flea from coming in and sitting down on you."

"Talk to my landlord," Nathaniel instructs him, as he closes his eyes. It has been a long night. "But I don't think he'll listen to you, either."

"See you around," the burglar says, stepping quietly out.

As he goes, Nathaniel has, at last, a quick look at him, and he wills himself to remember the face in case he should ever see it again.

"See you around," Nathaniel replies as the burglar closes the door behind him. "Drop by again. Just knock next time." He could always use another acquaintance, even one who steals. Still, he latches the door.

5

THE NEXT MORNING Nathaniel calls Theresa. The phone rings and rings and rings. Perhaps she is resting up after her social exertions. Or is out in the library, foraging in the stacks. Or is still actively caressing someone, somewhere—the two of them guttering and moaning into the sheets followed by sweaty laughter, the sun rising over her arched back, her fingers in someone's mouth, her breasts damp from kisses, her thighs from semen. *Ah,* Nathaniel notes, *yes, here it is,* the poison of jealous erotic imagery, the first sign, the barbed hook in the heart. Theresa Theresa Theresa.

He drives down to the Broadway farmers' market, buys two large bags' worth of assorted vegetables, then takes them back to the People's Kitchen, a little storefront co-op hunger-relief project on Allen Street. The butterscotch VW Beetle wheezes and squeaks and groans as he parks out in front, where a hapless bush occupying a small square of embattled dirt strokes the passenger-side door when he squeezes into the space. The People's Kitchen stands next to an artist's studio and is a block down from Mulligan's Brick

Bar. The neighborhood—Allentown—has a pleasantly lazy urban squalor. Nathaniel carries the vegetables inside, turns up the heat, causing the radiators to clank, raises the shades in the front and back, and, with the radio on, starts chopping carrots and boiling water. The poor and hungry and various assorted street people usually drop in starting around three in the afternoon for a meal. Sometimes Nathaniel serves, but today he is assigned to chop and boil and stir and clean.

In Buffalo, real estate is so cheap that almost any collective can buy or lease property, and Nathaniel has joined this one, the Allentown Artists' & Culinary Alliance, not out of vague progressive ideals, but because he likes cooking and cleaning and serving, and because his soul has always thrived being around cast-off people—greaseballs and windbag artistes, hippies, losers, the poor and unwashed, and those with sociopolitical ambitions, the ones who forget to wear socks and who blow their noses on their shirtsleeves while making speeches. Besides, once when he was meditating over the direction of his life, the message came to him that he should do this work.

He knows about himself that all his charitable deeds are, at base, selfish. Such drudgery makes him feel better, lifting a dead weight off his soul and putting a lighter-than-air spiritual substance in its place.

Through the south-facing back kitchen window the sun shines cheerfully, an all-American sun, optimistic about everything. In Buffalo, the sun is a member in good standing of the Rotary Club. *Things,* the sun sings merrily, *will get better better better better better better better better better.* Nathaniel turns up the volume on the radio, tuned to the Buffalo NPR affiliate, in an effort to drown out the sun. They're playing Vaughan Williams's Fifth Symphony, the second movement, a demented scherzo of sea shanties interrupted by a sudden eerie calm evoking the approach of nothingness. Nathaniel knows his classical music: before she married Nathaniel's stepfather, his mother played it day and night at home and in the car. Now he can recognize anything in the standard classical repertoire, and this knowledge burdens him. The sun shuts up.

When Nathaniel's mother and stepfather were living in New York City, and he would return home from college during spring break and, later, during the summers, the sunlight had a curiously hard metallic sheen. On good spring days the light defined trees, buildings, and people alike with brilliant tactile clarity. Then, in late summer, like the old-time God of the ancients, enraged, the sun would melt down whatever it saw and start over again. In August, Nathaniel thought, the sopping gruesome heat in Manhattan liquefied the city. Someday the entire urban landscape would ooze into the Hudson. In New York, summer would be the season of doom.

By contrast, his childhood sun over Milwaukee tended to be Midwestern and diffident, hidden by clouds tossed up by moisture from the Great Lakes. For most of his youth, he had lived under vague, noncommittal skies, broken occasionally by raging storms. Then the clouds would part to reveal the banal blue immensity.

His parents had resided in a three-bedroom suburban house with a white picket fence and a large grassy backyard with a rose garden, an arbor, and a reflecting ball, and to this day Nathaniel believes that if his father hadn't died of a sudden stroke in his forties, and if his sister hadn't been in the automobile accident that took her speech away, he would still be living out there in the suburbs, selling insurance or working as an accountant, starting a family and following some harmless occupation under those noncommittal Midwestern skies. He'd have a white picket fence and a rose garden of his own and a very white wife; he'd have an indistinct human outline and would genially fade into his home and family and belongings.

He cleans and cuts up the carrots and sets to work on the potatoes. The beef and celery can wait. The Vaughan Williams symphony progresses into its third movement, a meditative adagio.

During his lifetime, Nathaniel's father had run an elaborate charade: he gave the appearance of being just a standard-issue dad—a person you didn't have to pay much attention to. An astoundingly unremarkable man, display-case ordinary, an estate-planning attorney who worked at a law firm in downtown Milwaukee, he played catch with his son on weekends or did household repairs while he hummed the same tunes over and over again, "Blue Moon" or "Where or When." Clumsy and not a true handyman, he was nevertheless willing to repair anything if asked, carrying up his toolbox from the basement and laughing, "Look out, house! I'm coming!" He told jokes around the dinner table. In the morning he would playfully bonk his sleepy son on the head with the rolled-up newspaper to wake him. He would go fishing with his friends on Lake Winnitonka. As an alumnus of the University of Michigan, he watched Wolverine football on Saturdays if he had the time. He made of himself a generic parent, sweet and well-meaning and doubtlessly in a consensual relationship with routine. If he harbored quiet desperation, he kept it to himself.

After his death, he acquired perfection. Perfection dropped like an alarming protective covering over his memory, as Nathaniel and Catherine, his son and daughter, helplessly recognized—they saw it happen. No one could remember their father's flaws. Once he was gone, his benign imperturbable self became painfully lovable and thus toxic. His monkey way of scratching his back, his unpleasant habit of picking his teeth after dinner, his insistence on pouring too much garlic salt over the steaks before he grilled them, that strange equanimity of his—he never seemed to get angry, irritability being all he could manage—all of it coalesced into the composite of an affable man who, in everyone's collective memory, gave nobody the advantage of having a case against him. He had been sweet and generous. Who had noticed? Nobody. His virtues came back, as virtues will, to haunt the living.

He had taken his children for walks on trails through the city parks and into the playgrounds, where he had pushed them on the swings. He had carried first Catherine and then Nathaniel, as kids, on his shoulders; they had grabbed on to his hair to stabilize themselves and to steer him. He remembered birthdays, took the family on excursions to movies, and always showed up for school functions. He was a patiently good man who seemed to relish his nonentity status, his lack of individuality. Nathaniel on the basketball team, Catherine in gymnastics: he was there to witness them both. His habit of saying, "You've enlightened me." The beer after dinner, the affectionate kisses on the top of the head, his patience in teaching his kids how to swim or to ride a bicycle or to approach the net, his interest in history and Russian nineteenth-century fiction, his demand on New Year's Eve that his wife sit in his lap—oh, it was unforgivable, all of it, the entire inventory, it was a fortress that could never be breached once he was gone.

After her father's death, Catherine, silent and spectral, would sleepwalk into Nathaniel's bedroom. She would clear away his discarded clothes on the floor. Then she would descend, convulsed with sobs, and curl up like a dog. Already half a ghost herself, she brought herself to her brother's room so that he might witness her grief. If there had been consolation to be offered, Nathaniel had no idea where to find it. Their father, a genial guy they had taken for granted, was now fully absent and had taken all comfort with him. What was there to say? Nothing much. Nathaniel resorted to patting his sister on the back as she lay there on the floor beside his bed.

She had been a strong solid smart girl, with brilliant blue eyes that had ice traces in them. As a field hockey player and a rock singer fronting a high school band called Strep Throat, she had been good at raising her voice. With her particular appetites and raucousness, she would have been loved early on in the ordinary course of things by some brave boy who might have noticed and admired her. She was an inventory-taker, a psychic accountant, habitually noting quantities and qualities in rooms and in people. But after her father's death, a single inventory took over the others. "There was only one of him," she would sigh, over and over again.

She formed a new appetite for oblivion.

Nathaniel had not guessed that his sister could be furtive, brazenness having been her usual tactic, but, freed from stability, she developed a gift for secrecy. She joyfully took up drinking, a habit for which she had a calling. Alcoholism brought out her stealthy side, the midnight joy of beer from the refrigerator and whiskey from the cupboard. Nothingness called to her and she answered. At first she drank alone or with strangers. Her mother concealed all the liquor bottles—a guileless woman, she first tried hiding them behind the detergent boxes in the laundry room, where they were as obvious as Easter eggs—before throwing all of them out.

Catherine quickly found a community of like-minded high school classmates who drank, a whole crowd of fellow students who loved getting wasted as much as she herself did. They drank and drove and staggered around the woodsy Wisconsin off-road locales they found, cursing the sky, vomiting, laughing, falling down, passing out, waking up, and crawling behind the wheel before starting up the collaborating cars and weaving their way back.

On a Friday night in early November in Catherine's senior year, one of these boys, on a mission to take Catherine home, drove off the road into a patiently waiting tree. The impact threw her forward into the dashboard. When she came to, wrapped in swaddling clothes after several days of unconsciousness, all her words had been wiped clean from her brain's left hemisphere. She had sustained a skull fracture, a broken arm, and her body seemed to be one large bruise. The driver, a boy contemptuous of the future, had successfully canceled his own, but she had been saved—that is, her physical life had been saved—and before very long she was up and about, seemingly as beautiful as ever, except for her eyes, which had gone blank. The neurologists claimed that something had happened in her posterior temporal lobe, and they engaged in professional mumbling about the prognosis, saying that there would certainly be more tests until that stage when they could discover the source of her asymptomatic verbal aphasia. The tests, they said to Nathaniel and his mother, were very good these days. *We have excellent tests,* they said proudly, brain injury is no longer the grave mystery it once was, we will figure it out. And we have therapies, many of which have been proven to work. We are scientists; this is a *science.*

With her light dimmed, Catherine came home. She took up her life, almost, where it had been left off.

Around that time, Nathaniel began to notice ghost-women watching him from street corners, alleyways, from behind jewelry displays, ash-women, silent, mute, and un-moving, women trying on hats, women before mirrors, women deep in shadows, called forth in some manner by his sister's silence, called forth by the song of her injury to sur-round him and stare at him and accompany him everywhere. What did they want of him? They seemed ready to ask him a crucial question, these familiars, but they never got around to it. All through his college years, they kept up their surveil-lance. They stayed on their street corners with their hooded beautiful eyes, women-beggars made of mist and fog. They had moved into his world for good, it seemed, but they could not be spoken to—they always disappeared when he approached them. Often they opened their mouths to sing to him, though nothing audible ever came out. They were frequently bent over, human question marks, first in Mil-waukee and then in New York, after his mother remarried.

6

NATHANIEL LOOKS UP. There's one of them, right out in front, in broad sunlight. A woman wearing a blue denim cap, and a hideous pink cardigan sweater over a blouse with a printed pattern of marsh grass and bamboo, and purple slacks with threads of string for a belt—this apparition is staring in through the front window at him, her accusing eyes crazily fixed. She reaches up and takes out her teeth. She waves the dental plate at him. Hi! Hi hi hi hi hi. Ha ha ha ha ha ha ha ha. She flashes a startling bedlamite grin through the glass. She screams a fun-house laugh. Sometimes they do these stunts just to scare him, to watch the hair on the back of his neck stand up, to give him goose bumps. They like that. But they also have some other, undiscovered, agenda. He looks down at the table, where he has been chopping onions. Another pair of hands has joined his, another member of the Allentown Artists' & Culinary Alliance here in the People's Kitchen, one of his favorites, Jamie the Catholic—apparently she snuck in while he was hypnotized by that ghoul out there on the sidewalk. Having tied her apron on over a t-shirt and jeans, Jamie has set to work on shelling peas. Gold dangles from her earlobes. She is a lesbian and a sculptor and a dancer who lives in the neighborhood, and she drives a taxi for Queen City Cab at night to pay the bills, and Nathaniel loves her strong tanned forearms and blond flyaway frizzy hair poking out from under the contrivance of her head scarf (he also loves her soul), and he says in a formally affectionate tone, "Sweet Jamie. Good morning. How you doing?"

"How I doing? I doing all right. It's almost afternoon, dummy," she tells him, knocking her hip gently against Nathaniel's. "You should buy a watch. I slept late. I'm *so* bad. I'm a bad bad girl. Where's the rosemary?"

"Up on the shelf." He nods. "Close to the garlic. *You* know where it is." She reaches up to a shelf underneath a sign that says ANARCHISTS, PLEASE WASH YOUR HANDS! Tears squeeze out of his eyes. "Fucking onions. Always do this to me."

"Fucking onions," she agrees, shaking her head so that her earrings glitter. "You know what causes all that crying, don't you? Sulfur. Sulfur in the onion's oil. The devil's molecule. Aren't you going to ask me why I slept late?"

"Okay. Jamie, why'd you sleep late?"

"None of your damn business, Nathaniel." She grins. "I got lucky. So how come you didn't sleep late?"

"I *didn't* get lucky." He's about to tell her about the burglar but decides not to; she'd be alarmed on his behalf.

"You poor child. Why didn't you get lucky?"

He stops slicing for a moment. "Is there accounting for luck? Anyway, this girl said that if she was ever going to go to bed with me, she wanted to be sober."

"Sober! To sleep with a man, you'd *have* to be drunk. What a crock. Sober! Don't believe her. Girls are such liars. Well, maybe she wants to know you better. Maybe she wants to know your *sign*. Your *horoscope*. If you love *cats*. If you can *commit*. Hey, aren't you going to ask me," she asks, "about who made me late?"

"So, Jamie," he says, "who made you late?"

"None of your business." She laughs loudly. "Check the society pages. Jesus, I wonder if we have mice in here. I saw rodent leavings when I came in. Back there near the door, while you were staring at the front window? Somebody should clean up the rear entryway. You, probably. It's your assignment today, isn't it? Man, I think this is serious, the mice problem, I mean."

"Of course we have mice." He glances at the front window, where the toothless woman has dissolved into the noontime air of Buffalo. "And, yeah, I ought to put out some traps before the city shuts us down."

"They'll shut us down anyway. Any day now. Pronto. They hate us. Free food is a thumb in the eye of free enterprise, is what they think. People hate charity; they really do. It insults the worker. The city will come in with inspectors and cops and tear gas, and it'll be curtains for us." Jamie looks down at his crotch, hidden by his own apron. "You know, babycakes, you're kinda cute, for a guy," she says. "Listen. Don't take this wrong. I'm serious. If you're lonely and need a sleepmate," she says quietly, almost in a whisper, "give me a call. I'm not kidding. I wouldn't mind holding you all night. You have virtues, and virtues," she says, slicing into another carrot, "should be rewarded, occasionally, with kindness."

"You're so romantic," Nathaniel says.

"Romance is in my nature." After a pause of chopping and seasoning, Jamie asks, "What was her name? *Is* her name?"

"Theresa. We were at a party."

Jamie nods twice, frowning, and seems ready to speak up when the phone rings. Nathaniel wipes his hands before answering it. "Thank you," the voice says without benefit of a greeting, "for taking me home." For a moment, Nathaniel can't place the voice as young or old, male or female, or even human, can't place it at all until he realizes that it belongs, if that's the word, to Coolberg.

"Ah. Jerome," Nathaniel says, as the Vaughan Williams on the radio behind him embarks on its finale, a very British passacaglia with brave launching-into-the-void sentiments. "How'd you know I was here?"

"Don't you remember last night?" Coolberg asks. "I told you: *I know everything about you.* You were a little drunk and got . . . I don't know, confessional. You said you worked at the People's Kitchen on Saturday mornings, preparing meals for the poor. Very admirable. That's what you *said.* So I called. Don't you remember? That was right after you told me about your sister and your father . . ."

"I did? I talked about them? I don't think I said anything about them."

"Well, I certainly *thought* you did." A pause. "Your father's death? From a stroke? Your sister's muteness? How she slept on the floor beside your bed after your dad died? Your mother's brief spell of unreason?"

Nathaniel waits. Someone in the world claims, on very little evidence, to know everything about him. Despite his doubts, he feels flattered. He notices that Jamie has turned around and is watching him, studying him as if he needs protection from something scratching through the wall.

"It's just that I was thinking," says Coolberg, "that we should do something together. I mentioned this to you. Possibly you forgot. We should go see the gods come out. At night. At Niagara Falls. Have you ever done that? Ever seen the gods come out? You should. They're quite a sight, the gods."

"No, I haven't." He waits. "What's this about the gods? I never heard of any. Besides God, I mean."

"Oh, skepticism is so easy, Nathaniel. And *lazy*. Lazily uninteresting. This excursion—we should do it. The pagan gods have a new boldness. They desire to be seen. The name of God is changing in our time. Really. Don't you agree? Besides, you have a car. I don't drive. I have *never* driven. With me, practice doesn't make perfect. I have no sense of direction."

"Okay. But we should bring Theresa along, you know? If I'm going to take an excursion, it should be the three of us."

In the long silence that follows, Jamie has shrugged and returned to washing and chopping and tossing vegetables into the stewpot. "Yes," Coolberg says at last. "What a good idea. You call her. When do you want to go?"

"How about tomorrow night? It's Sunday. The gods come out on Sunday, don't they? It's their day, Sunday. Right?"

"Fine," Coolberg says angrily. Nathaniel hears the telltale *click* of the disconnection. Apparently Coolberg never says hello *or* good-bye.

When he returns to Jamie's side, she asks him who it was, and when he tells her, she puts down her knife, drops her hands to her sides, and slowly leans sideways into him, a gesture of affection and, it seems—Nathaniel can't be sure—protection. "I should be your guardian angel," she says. "I think you need one." She drops her head on his shoulder for a split second. Under the protective chef's head scarf, her blond hair brushes against his neck. It *feels* blond.

"Do you know that guy who called me? Coolberg?"

"No," she tells him. "It was the look on your face I recognized."

"What look?"

"Like you were being pickpocketed. Or, I dunno, *taken*. You make me nervous," Jamie tells him. "You're too available. You need to be more vigilant. Close yourself down a little. Men shouldn't be like you. Give me a call, if you ever think of it."

7

JUST BEFORE HE LEAVES in the early afternoon, Nathaniel, who has finished mopping and disinfecting the floor near the kitchen drain, sees a guy escorting a pregnant woman, evidently his wife, through the front door and then to one of the long community tables. She walks past the entryway in deliberate stages, first limping from a bad left knee, then waving brokenly with her right arm for balance, as if she were directing traffic. Her progress comes in physical-therapy steps. Apparently she doubts that she will stay upright. Regaining her dignity, she sits down slowly before gazing at the dining area with the abstracted air of a queen about to announce a decree. Her husband—they are both wearing wedding rings—is white, and she is black, though their facial features are rather similar, with dark widely spaced eyes, Italian, as if they had both descended from the Medicis, one side in Italy, the other in Africa. It is the burglar and his wife, and when the burglar sees Nathaniel he nods, very quickly, a hi-but-don't-come-over-here look.

When Nathaniel approaches them, the burglar glares at

him, resisting. Nathaniel walks through his resistance. He says, "Hi. I'm Nathaniel." He holds out his hand.

"Um, it's Ben," the burglar says, referring to himself. He gestures in his wife's direction. "This here's Luceel."

"Hi, Luceel," Nathaniel says. Luceel gazes at him before studying her hands in her lap. She has great physical beauty and will not exchange more than a quick once-over with just anybody. She is one of those women who rations out her glances. Maybe she is just shy.

"Um, hi. You two know each other?" she asks, looking at her fingers.

"We've met," Ben says. "That's all it is. We met someplace. He remembers me from a thing we did." He sighs loudly, examining the traffic passing outside and shaking his head, as if the mere fact of the cars oppresses him, all those Buicks, Chevrolets, and Fords, with their purposeful owners.

"Right," Nathaniel says. "Well. See you later. Nice to meet you, Luceel. Have a good afternoon, you guys."

As he walks out the front door, he notices that they are conferring together, heads lowered, this topic having momentarily taken precedence over food and hunger.

In the afternoon he plays basketball in a city park with a group of guys he's seen here before, most of them about his size, their elbows as aggressive as his own, their collective breath visibly rising above them in the cold autumn air, their sweat soaking through their shirts. One basket has a chain net hanging from the hoop; the other hoop, on the opposite court, is naked, with an unpadded support pole holding up the backboard—a funky urban playground for adults, inmates of the city. Nathaniel plays slowly and distractedly, but the other players, too, have strangely mournful expressions on their weekend faces, like the little men bowling in "Rip Van Winkle" who were unable to smile. Despite their gloom they all make self-encouraging male noises, and the noises free them. Doing a lay-up, Nathaniel allows himself a loud triumphant outcry.

The ball falls neatly through the hoop.

Back in his apartment after his shower, he gets Theresa on the line, and her apologies begin, one by one. Apologies? For what? She launches in with her mistakes in tone, advances to mistakes in behavior, and ends with the full self-indictment. "I'm a total fraud. Somebody should arrest me," she says calmly. "Last night? That wasn't me." The confession of fraudulence sounds fraudulent, though it has charm. Nathaniel notices that she speaks quietly, intimately. Listening to her is like being in a sensual confessional booth across the hall from a hot steamy bedroom. Her statements emerge from her full of self-doubt, the sweetly narcissistic self-censorious note struck again and again, as if she is surprised to find that she actually likes him a bit more than she likes herself and is evoking her own dubious flaws so that he can refute her, thus showering her with praise and returning the conversation to the subject of her wonderful, winning self.

"See, the thing is," she tells him, and then trails off into strategic mumbling. She admits her yearning to inhabit an intellectual realm that she has not by rights acquired citizenship to. "Oh, everyone else around here is so smart," she confesses, "and all I can do is to put on an act." Really, she says, she is just a simple girl brought up in buttfuck Iowa, the daughter of a manufacturer's rep who sold prefabricated silos. She's afraid of being dumb, a silo salesman's daughter—that's her breathy assertion.

She has mastered somehow a tonal mixture of the bogus

and the seductive, so Nathaniel interrupts. "But you were quoting Valéry last night!" he says. "Who else does that?"

"That line, that's the one line I know," she says. "That one. I always quote it. '*Beau ciel, vrai ciel, regard-moi qui change!*' That gets me in the door, that line, it's the key to the city."

"Okay. Enough. You know something? When we came in last night," Nathaniel says, before a coughing fit takes him over, "everyone thought we were a couple."

"Yeah? You think so? Why?"

"Because they said so. Because we were both soaked. Because we looked it. There was a perception there. Of, what's that word? Togetherness. That we were mated."

"Yeah?" She waits. "Well, who knows? It *could* happen. You and me, I mean. I'd just have to dump my boyfriend. I'd have to cheat on him. Of course, that's always a possibility. Sometimes I *do* despise him. He lives in Berkeley, half a million miles away. And, after all, he's an out-and-out android, this guy. Robby. Robby the Robot."

"So let me ask you a question," Nathaniel says, improvising. "There's something I can't remember about what happened when I drove you home. Did I talk about my father and my sister last night? Coolberg said I did."

"Oh, him. Hell, I don't know. I didn't hear you saying anything like that. Forget him, all right?"

"All right. Sure. But I can't forget him—he just called. Listen: he wants to go to Niagara Falls tomorrow evening. *To see the gods come out,* is what he says. I told him I wouldn't go unless I brought you along. Can you come?" To break the pause that follows, he asks, "*Will* you come? You've got to."

"All right," she says. "Yes. But what's all this about the gods? *What* gods?"

"How should I know? I'm not acquainted with them. You should ask him."

"Nathaniel," she says.

"What?"

"Take me somewhere. Right now. Okay? Come get me and take me somewhere. I'm alone here and I can't stand it and I need to be delivered. I've been drinking stale burned coffee and having a breakdown. The kind where you tear paper into little strips and then stare at the phone? And you watch the sun crossing the sky? A day with no future? That kind."

"Where do you want to go?"

"No, no, don't ask me. I don't care. Uh, wait: I *do* care. Last night, you said something about the Mirrored Room. The one in the Albright-Knox? Floors, ceilings, walls—all mirrors? That Lucas Samaras piece. We could do a trip over there. We need a break. We could be trapped in infinity. That'd be cool. Come get me in that strange little car of yours and take me to the Mirrored Room, all right? You remember where I live?"

"Yeah," he says, hanging up in so much of a rush that he forgets to say good-bye to her, which is just what Coolberg does.

8

INSIDE LUCAS SAMARAS'S Mirrored Room, in his socks—once again, shoes must be left outside, and only two people can inhabit the room at one time—Nathaniel takes Theresa's hand. He is making an effort to think, but this site itself disposes of ideas quickly, leaving the visitor empty and somehow impaired. The question of whether this assembly is "art" seems somehow beside the point, though what that point may actually be recedes and dissolves like all other points, into the mirrors. The air in the Mirrored Room smells rank, a soiled and not-at-all-friendly unventilated stenchy atmosphere in three cavernous dimensions. This eight-foot cube has a table and chair inside, placed against the opposing wall, both objects with mirrored surfaces, opposite which the only available light trickles in from the doorway, and either the glass has been tinted, or infinity itself, as revealed by the mirrors, is green, a color that in this particular case has been emptied of all hope. The mirrored chair appears to be a joke and affords no rest to the visitor. Light inside the room, dog-tired, bounces off the surfaces until it drops.

Nathaniel has been warned by a friend: the visitor to this room returns to the rest of the museum uncertain whether he has had an interesting experience or a dull one or any experience at all. Nothing attaches to the room, and visitors are usually eager to escape its confines.

Looking down, Nathaniel sees himself and Theresa, holding hands, reflected so that they stand underneath the floor, balanced upside down on the images of themselves, as if under a layering of lake ice, the two of them submerged, immersed in glass, duplicating themselves in an arc traveling farther downward toward the lake's bottom, and, past that, into the earth's core. Above them and to the sides, their images pile up on top of each other, daisy-chained into a green velvety vertical sky-darkness. Everywhere he looks, Nathaniel sees himself—t-shirt, jeans, jacket, socks—attached by hand and thus umbilicaled to Theresa, similarly t-shirted, jeaned, jacketed, socked, their eyes perfectly aligned. He is looking at the mirrors, and Theresa trades that look with hers, and he looks at her looking at him looking at the mirrors.

But if mirrors multiply space, they must also multiply time. Nathaniel peers into the visual soup created by the green mirrorglass. There he is. He sees himself, having aged, eighteen reflections down, eighteen/twenty/thirty years from now, holding Theresa's hand. There he is, with her, in the disenchanted darkness, smaller, faded, old, a tiny bent nonagenarian. There he is, there *they* are, a particled assemblage of atoms and molecules; there they will be, aged, aging, in the mirrors, growing dark and gray and small, and, somewhere off in the temporal distance, pinpointed, exquisite human nebulae, dying and dead and then gone. He approaches the mirror to see what the expression on that person's face is years from now, that person being him-

self, though he can't see it—him—because the closer he
approaches the mirror, the more the distant images recede
into nothingness, blanked out by himself. He can see these
echoing images only if he stands away from them. From
there, they are like almost invisible light from distant stars
fueled by stone, flickering out.

"Nathaniel?" Theresa asks, grinning. The mirrors please
her. She makes a sudden little guttural noise.

He can't stand being in here; he can't breathe. This
room-sized speculum involves the domestication of the
infinite. And that's the least of it—the room feels disagree-
able and really quite monstrous, meant to undermine the
soul by wrapping it in reflections. And yet he smiles at her
and picks her up as if they had consummated a joyous occasion in this room, and he carries her out, back into the
adjoining day, a gray gallery of paintings safely held in their
two dimensions. He lowers her, and she touches him quickly
on the earlobe.

"That place made me wet. I started to come in there," she
says quietly, and it takes Nathaniel a moment before he
understands what she means and then another moment
before he can believe it, but when she offers him her tremu-
lous hand, the skin gives him a faint but distinct erotic
shock.

Unable to speak, he accompanies her to the car, takes her
home, walks her to her apartment above the ice-cream shop,
staying behind her as she seemingly floats up the stairs, his
hand snuggled in the back pocket of her jeans while she
unlocks the door and makes her way past the old vinyl-
covered chair near the phone, where he kisses her.

When he breaks the kiss, he says, "A burglar was in my
apartment last night."

She seems unmoved. "Did he take anything?"

"No," Nathaniel tells her. "I made him a cup of coffee. Anyway, he was only a burglar." Strips of paper have indeed been scattered everywhere in her despair, and beyond the window, the afternoon sun is sputtering out. The room has caught the odors of the waffle cones on the first floor, and the vanilla-candy confectionery smell is on Theresa's breath. Her cat, lying on top of a book of crossword puzzles, eyes Nathaniel with autistic worry and suspicion. Theresa leads him into the bedroom, where they spend the rest of the day and the evening. They forget to eat until long after dark.

"Don't get any ideas," she says, drowsy, her voice a flat-line, just before midnight, a few minutes after her last orgasm, when she has called out to Jesus again. "This doesn't mean that I like you. Let's not be sentimental." She smiles and pats him on the cheek. "But I sure did like our field trip. Time for you to go home, honey."

9

THE NEXT MORNING while he is making poached eggs
for himself, his sister calls, as she always does on Sunday
morning around ten o'clock. He knows Catherine's calls
from everyone else's because she never speaks. She just listens while he talks. He does his best to fill his sister in on his
life. The phone rings; he answers it. Silence from her. That's
their tradition.

"Hi, Catherine," he says into the dead roar of long distance. He never asks her anything because there's no point
in asking; she can't speak. How she can comprehend human
speech but not be able to speak herself? A neurological mystery. In any case, every Sunday he has to concoct a newsy
monologue for her. "So. I had a pretty good week. The
classes are going well. Nothing to complain about there,
really. It's been raining. Friday night I went to a party and
met this girl. Actually I'd met her before but we bumped
into each other again outside the party, and we went in
together. I took her home. And there was somebody else
there, at this party, this guy named Coolberg . . . I don't
really know who he is, but he claims to know all about me. I

don't know how he knows. Yesterday afternoon I played basketball with these guys who are usually at this park, and in the morning I worked in the People's Kitchen and . . . oh, I almost forgot to tell you. On Friday night I came home and there was a burglar in my apartment, but he was an okay guy and was stoned out of his mind and so I made coffee for him, and believe it or not, we almost became friends, maybe. So, anyway, yesterday I was working at the People's Kitchen, the one I've told you about, and the burglar and his wife came in, Ben and Luceel—that's their names. They introduced themselves. Funny coincidence. I don't know, Sis, sometimes I think my life is full of these strange . . . *happenings,* these weird events that just drop on me. They remind me of what Jung wrote about concerning coincidences. Carl Jung, the psychologist? *He* talked about how there are no real accidents. He could be right. And so anyway yesterday afternoon this girl I met on Friday—I called her, her name's Theresa, and we went over to the art museum here in town and went into a room that was made of mirrors, floor to ceiling. It made me feel, I don't know, sort of woozy, like I would pass out, like I'd disappear somehow. Then I took her back to her place. I have to study this afternoon, but tonight this girl, Theresa, and I are going out to Niagara Falls, with Coolberg, the one who says he knows me, to see the gods come out. Well, I mean, that's what he *calls* it. I don't really know what he means by that, but I guess I'll find out . . ."

Just beyond his apartment window an old woman who is pushing a grocery cart stops and stands on the sidewalk, staring in toward him.

"What the gods are, I mean. I thought they were all gone. Aren't they?"

A thought: What if this is not his sister on the phone?

What if he's talking and telling all this to someone else, not his sister at all, a terribly wrong number, someone who has happened to call him deliberately or by mistake, someone who doesn't say "Hello" or identify himself when you answer?

But Nathaniel continues to narrate the story of his recent life, into what he thinks is his sister's silence. After all, she needs his stories. She needs him to talk. The stories keep her alive, or so he believes.

10

ON THE WAY to Niagara Falls, at dusk, to see the gods come out, they cross Grand Island. Coolberg sits in the backseat, Theresa reclines on the passenger side, Nathaniel is hunched behind the wheel. They pass a little abandoned amusement park. The humble roller coaster is oxidizing gradually into scrap metal, and one loop-de-loop lies dead on the ground. Nathaniel imagines the joyful screams of yesteryear. Above the roar of the VW's engine, and to pass the time, Coolberg begins to describe a trip he apparently made last summer to a country whose name, when he says it, sounds like "Quolbernya," one of those rarely visited Eastern European locales at the edge of, or just off, the map.

"In that country," Coolberg says, in a voice that gradually gains momentum, "the houses are all built of white stone. They're sepulchral, these houses, like those in a Bergman movie, and although they have huge drooping gutters and oversized windows, nothing about them seems particularly *knowable*. The people there don't believe in directional signs, to begin with. They think you should know how to get where you're going, and you should always know where you already are. But by law, they require homeowners to plant decorative purple lilacs in their backyards, which will bloom throughout the seasons, lilacs engineered in the local laboratories so that not even snow will kill them. Another thing I noticed was that families no longer go down to the docks to welcome the passengers, because people have become, without anyone knowing why, too much trouble. The waves flatten out oddly in the central harbor, which is obscurely brokenhearted, like Lisbon. It's one of those places that history currently ignores. The sights extrude a kind of nineteenth-century pain. There is nevertheless much actuality. The state planning makes everyone feel like a miniature, and though I found a few maps printed on high-quality paper, the maps themselves were fictional, and comically inaccurate. And, after all, people were indifferent to exact location—or they didn't 'care,' if that's the word—and I noticed that at dinnertime they bent down to their plates, where invariably food was located, and most of them ate and didn't remark upon where they were."

He takes a breath and makes a sound like a giggle. Nathaniel feels rage, a rare emotion for him, rising up at this mockery of eloquence and distinction-making, this travelogue through a massive cognitive disorder, this manic word-spinning, but before he can interrupt, Coolberg starts in again.

"Everyone's very loyal to the directives, for example, about eating the food. It's one of those countries where people are particularly loyal to *loyalty*. Also, there's the business of sleeping, how much dreaming has to be done, who has to love whom, that sort of thing. Their murders are elaborately planned and executed. Nothing is left to chance. As they like to say there, 'You certainly have to dream a lot of dreams to get through a lifetime.' In the capital city, I went to the pavilion of end-of-the-world horticulture. The plain-faced plant-woman sprinkled powerful dust on the flowers for my benefit and explained that the long fields where nothing will grow that we had spied from the tourist buses, and the rivers that had turned to the color of cough drops, were not really manifestations of anything disarrayed in the organic world, understood as such. She said everything was demonstrably mending. She was almost alone in the pavilion. Her voice echoed, in that bottom-of-the-well manner. *Trust me,* the plain-faced woman said. And then in French, *Oui, je la connais.* But if I was supposed to trust her, to acknowledge that she knew something, then why were all the children in the neighboring playground so frightened, their mouths making those terrible O's? Why wouldn't the lilacs stop blooming? Why did the gifts hurt long after they'd been given? *Those* were the questions. One morning I knew, finally, that the lists of examples wouldn't do any longer, but *examples were all that I had.* In that country, they speak prose. And not only do they speak it, they live it. They didn't ban poetry—they still encourage it, officially—but they did get rid of the insides of things, the interiors that poetry once, in another era, before the fall, referred to. In that sense, they are like us." He says the last sentence almost in a whisper, a loud whisper over the engine noise, as if confiding his single precious insight.

"Would you please shut the fuck up?" Nathaniel shouts.

"Oh, okay," Coolberg says, smilingly exhausted after his riff. "I just wanted to tell you about the Quolbernyans." He waits for a moment before saying, "And about those lilacs? The ones that never die."

"Jeez," Theresa says. "Where did you get *that* routine? I thought I knew them all."

"I was reciting a poem," Coolberg says modestly. "Almost."

"Well, don't ever do it again," warns Nathaniel, gripping the steering wheel. "It's like vomiting in front of people." They pass over the second bridge from Grand Island and turn onto Buffalo Avenue, running parallel to the Robert Moses Parkway, which leads to Niagara Falls on the American side.

"Who's been out here?" Nathaniel asks. "To the falls?"

"Well, I never have," Theresa informs him.

"Me neither," Coolberg tells them quietly, seemingly miffed.

"How'd you know about the gods, then? That was the whole *point* of this expedition. 'Gods' are what you promised," Theresa says.

"I had heard about them," Coolberg explains. "From someone. Someone who had seen them. Besides, look." He points ahead. A smell from the atmosphere invades the car's interior, filling the little Volkswagen with the odor of petrochemical solvents. On the left-hand side along Buffalo Avenue is an array of chemical plants, visible ahead along the river for miles: DuPont, Carborundum, Olin, Dow, Occidental Chemical, others, all brightly lit in gold by sodium-vapor lamps. The plants' complicated tubular pipes look like giant industrial webbing connected to enormous black-and-gray fortress-refineries and processing machinery, their smokestacks decorated with evenly spaced vertical lights and red blinking stars at the top—lighthouses that beckon the chemical storm and resist it. Close to them are gas flares. This display is the triumph of something that does not want to be named. No humans are visible, no cars are parked. Nothing appears to be moving except for the smoke that wafts like a little industrial storm cloud toward the parkway, the Niagara River, and the car in which they are traveling. A background hum is audible. This entire complex operates without any human intervention and could continue forever without anyone turning a dial or throwing a switch. Nevertheless, Coolberg is correct: some presence is here. You can hear it.

"Valhalla," Coolberg says, from the backseat.

"Should we stop?" Theresa asks.

"Stop? Stop where?"

"Well, anywhere." She shakes her head. "To go in. Nobody works here, that's obvious. These factories are all automa-tized. Is that the word? Automated. *That's* the word. They run themselves. No one's been here in years." She puts her hands under her armpits for warmth. She shivers and grins. She is so beautiful when she shivers; she shivers and trembles when she comes.

"There are fences and barriers and guard shacks. The lights have to be replaced. See those KEEP OUT signs?" Nathaniel asks, ever the practical soul.

"Xanadu," Coolberg says from the backseat. "Stately plea-sure domes."

Nathaniel takes an angry left turn onto a service drive, downshifts into second, then takes another turn into a mostly vacant parking lot bordering a squat brick building over whose doorway are the words THE CARBORVNDVM COMPANY. Behind them, and at a distance, a ghostly train consisting of chemical tankers chugs forward into the dark-ness. In the lot where they have parked, tanker trucks rumble, their engines still running as they do at freeway rest stops, though Nathaniel cannot see their drivers. In the dis-tance, a siren wails, then abruptly cuts off in mid-shriek.

"Want to get out of the car?" Nathaniel asks. "Take a tour?"

"What do they make here?" Theresa asks him.

"Snack food."

"Polyester fire-retardant snack food."

"All right, all right. That's enough of that duet." Nathaniel's foot taps nervously on the brake pedal. "Do we get out? Do we take a safari into one of these places?"

Theresa looks straight at him. "You're kidding, right? Listen, I just changed my mind. If they found us here, they'd kill us. They'd douse us with their chemical compounds and set us on fire. No, no, this isn't where we're supposed to be. This place is creepy, Nathaniel. We must *exit*. We must drive *away*."

As they are talking, a night watchman wearing a blue Pinkerton uniform emerges from a small shed attached to one of the larger buildings. The door he opens is rusty, as is the shed, and a red rust attaches itself to the gravel he steps on. His red hair leaves the impression that rust has attached itself to his body as well, slowly burning him from the inside out and from the top down. He makes his way in a leisurely cop-saunter over to where their car is idling. He has perfected the tough coolness of an enforcer, even though he seems to have no gun, only a billyclub. When he reaches their car, Nathaniel lowers his window, and the guard, whose hair is even rustier when viewed close-up, and whose face has the humid florid flush of youthful high blood pressure, bends down to ask, "What're you folks doing here? This is private property. You got business here?"

"That's not the god," Coolberg says. "He's a fake."

The night watchman glances at him, or, rather, one eye does. The other eye does not move. It appears to be made of glass.

"We were just leaving," Nathaniel says, starting the car and then throwing it into reverse. He backs out, narrowly missing one of the snoring semi-trailer trucks, and returns to Buffalo Avenue.

11

AFTER PARKING THE VW, they make their way across a footbridge to Goat Island, Nathaniel in the lead like a Boy Scout. The park closes at eleven, according to a sign they have passed near a vacant squad car that has the words PARK ANGER on it, the decal R in RANGER having been removed or painted over by some vandal. On the east tip of the island, they find a bench and sit down, Theresa in the middle, facing the Niagara River as it divides on their left toward the American rapids and on their right toward Horseshoe Falls. A few scraggly leafless maples stand on either side of them, the falls roaring melodramatically just out of sight behind them.

In the wind, the streetlights vibrate and chatter.

"What are we doing here?" Theresa asks, her voice coming out in a nervous squeak. "Here in this stupid park?" She waits, and when neither of the men answers, she says, "Don't say 'gods.' That's just the cover story."

"Of course the gods are here," Coolberg says. "Why do you think newlyweds come to this place?" He pauses. "They want to partake. They want to share in the god-stuff." He turns his head to stare at Nathaniel, who is gazing out at the water.

In the midst of his reverie, Nathaniel does not remember why he agreed to this expedition. Following the path to this part of the island, they had walked past the statue of Nikola Tesla, inventor of alternating current and the death ray, who claimed, late in his madness, that he could split the earth in half like an apple. Behind their bench on the other side of Goat Island are the modest tourist traps for visitors: Ripley's Believe It Or Not! Museum, the Daredevil Museum, and Louis Tussaud's Waxworks. The bench is uncomfortable and gives him a slatted pain in his shoulder blades. Someday, he thinks, he'll chalk this trip up to the adventurousness of youth and high spirits. But for now . . . what? Gradually his eyes adjust to the darkness. A small crowd of Japanese tourists passes behind them, snapping flash photos in the dark.

Something terrible is about to happen. The thought drifts downward over him like a veil over a face. And at that moment, he reflects that some people, like Coolberg, simply have a talent that he himself lacks—a talent for creating hypothetical narratives out of the air, out of nothing. *Gods.* If you play a tune, a few suckers will always dance to it. But first you have to play the tune and, even before that, advertise the concert. No tune, no dancing. What an innocent I am, he thinks.

The fact of water rushing past in the river; the fact of the rich fetid darkness in this park, at night; the fact of a few storm clouds and a bit of lightning; the fact of beautiful, anxiously intelligent Theresa sitting next to him, who may or may not now be his adoring lover—all these facts make him uneasy. Ease? Ease is elsewhere. Ease is for others.

When, Nathaniel wonders, will I ever get free of these narratives in which the gods are promised? When will anybody?

"Nothing is going to happen," he says glumly. "Nothing is ever going to happen."

"Oh, yes," Coolberg says, his voice coming out of the dark. "Something will. Something will always happen. You just have to wait patiently until it does."

"And how long is that?" asks Theresa.

"*We* can make it happen," Coolberg says, chuckling. "History is ours. For example." He rises from the bench and shambles in his raincoat over to where the water laps against Goat Island. Theresa and Nathaniel follow him. Down below, the Niagara River seems to be calm, but, under the surface, probably isn't. If you fell in that water, there would be no resisting it. All your earthly choices would be over.

"The gods are in the water," Coolberg says. "That's why they have the dynamo over there, down below, to capture them." He waits for a minute. "People think that the gods are in the air, but they aren't. They're pulsating down below. They're waterborne. Then they're pushed by the generators into high power lines. Okay. I have an idea."

"What's your idea?" Nathaniel asks.

"I'll stand here," Coolberg says. "With my back to you, with me facing the river. And what you do is, you push me, and I'll start to fall into the river, and then, after I've lost my balance but just before I fall, you reach out and you grab me. You pull me back."

"I don't like your idea," Theresa says.

"Well, it's a serious idea, and here I am," Coolberg tells her, walking forward a few steps toward the embankment, where the park service has cleared away the scrub brush for the sake of the view. The distance to the water seems negligible, but it's impossible to tell how deep the river might be here. He holds his arms out in a gesture of resignation, a shrug, or an imitation of a crucifixion, an homage to the gods he has claimed are located in this spot. In front of them, the river flows past, dividing. "Grab on to my coat," he shouts.

Nathaniel takes a handful of cloth at midlevel in his right fist and another handful, lower, in his left. Then he unclutches his hands, letting Coolberg go.

"Okay," Coolberg says. "Theresa," he says, "push me into the river."

Theresa looks down at her shoes. "Aren't we too old for this?" she asks. "Aren't we adults by now?"

"Give me a push."

There is a moment when everything stops. Nathaniel glances up to see the masses of land in the distance—Grand Island and Navy Island. A late-autumn thunderstorm has opened the heavens with cumulonimbus clouds and lightning. As if in slow motion, Theresa gives Coolberg a tentative push, and Coolberg loses his balance. He appears to tilt forward yearningly toward the water and his own death, and at that point, Nathaniel, almost without thinking, lunges toward him. With one hand he grabs the back of his coat and with his left arm encircles Coolberg's waist, pulling him back onto safe ground, while in the distance cloud lightning briefly illuminates the scene.

"Thank you. I've been saved. Your turn," Coolberg says to Theresa. He turns to Nathaniel. "See? Something happened. It's like a drug that wakes you up."

Nathaniel expects Theresa to balk, but she doesn't. She stands exactly where Coolberg stood, though she does not hold her arms out as he did, in the crucifixion shrug. Nathaniel cannot see her face clearly, but he can tell that her eyes are closed.

"Okay, I'm ready," she says.

"I'll do this," Nathaniel announces, slipping in behind her. With his right arm, he gives her a slight push but with insufficient force to cause her to lose her balance or to fall forward. She does lean over, pantomiming a fall, as his arm clutches her just above the hip as a lover would, whereupon she falls backward into him, as if she knew all along that this stunt was a pretext for some good-natured fun. Somehow both his arms surround her now as if he were embracing her—no, not "as if," because that's actually what he's doing, he realizes, as she squirms. She turns around and lifts her face to kiss him, standing on tiptoes, a quick kiss that he returns. Coolberg is of course watching this.

"Would you kiss her again?" he asks. "I'd like to see that."

"No," Nathaniel whispers angrily. "For Christ's sake."

"In that case, it's your turn."

Reluctantly, in a kind of dream state, Nathaniel releases Theresa to take his place in front of the embankment. *Someone has always saved me,* he thinks as he closes his eyes. When his father died and his sister lost her words, and his beautiful mother seemed about to be as unstable as a canoe in white water, his stepfather took over their care and removed the family to New York, to the sunny apartment on West End Avenue, walking distance to the overpraised Zabar's. Life settled down long enough for him to grow to be a man and for his mother to regain her steady calm heart. For an instant, he remembers the rug in the doorway of his stepfather's apartment on the eleventh floor of the building, its deep red weave.

Through his closed eyelids, he stares at the darkness before him. He listens to the water for a five-second eternity. Then two hands push at him, he begins to fall forward, and nothing reaches out at his sweater to pull him back. Nothing saves him.

12

LIFE IS A SERIES of anticlimaxes until the last one. Standing in the Niagara River with the water up to his waist, Nathaniel turns to see his friends. They are standing on the bank watching him, and Theresa may be screaming in laughter, but in the onrushing river noise, he can't hear her; Coolberg continues to stare at him, or so it appears when the lightning illuminates the scene. If he loses his balance now, he'll be gone forever, of course; he'll be swept away. Why did they think that the river just off Goat Island would be over their heads? It's nighttime and the water is dirty— they couldn't see.

Nevertheless, he can't move.

13

IN THE CAR heading back to Buffalo, Nathaniel says nothing. He has no observations to make about how he stepped gingerly back to the island, nothing to comment upon to either Coolberg or Theresa about their inability to reach out for him, no sly remarks about their collective intentions.

"Okay," Coolberg says. "If you're not going to say anything to us, do you mind if we turn on the radio?"

Theresa twists the knob, and a Buffalo station floats up into the car's noisy silence. They're playing the Beach Boys' "God Only Knows."

The unearthly beauty of the music fills the car. Nathaniel listens: muted horns, strings, tapped blocks, sleigh bells, a linear vocal line lightly harmonized in thirds until, three-quarters of the way through, the music becomes vertical rather than horizontal, as the voices pile up in a series of increasingly complicated harmonies in a refrain—*God only knows what I'd be without you*—repeated and repeated and repeated, with a frightening emphasis on the word "what," until the voices fade out, having absolutely nowhere to go.

This is the song, Nathaniel knows, in which Brian Wilson handed over his heart to God and simultaneously lost his mind. The song is Brian Wilson's favorite, the one he sold his soul for. After "God Only Knows" there were other songs, certainly, "Good Vibrations" and the rest of them, but the spirit had abandoned him: addressed not to a California girl, a sun-bleached surfer-chick, the refrain had been spoken to his own spirit, his genius, which, in one of those ironies of which life is so fond, left him there and then.

"Okay, I'll talk to you," Nathaniel says, turning the volume down, and both Coolberg and Theresa sigh with relief.

"So. How did you like the gods?" Coolberg asks.

"Would you stop with this talk about the gods, please? They were roaring," he replies. "Anyway, what difference does it make?"

"Oh, hypothetically, it doesn't make—"

"'Hypothetically.' That's an interesting word, considering what we just did. Hypothetically, I could have just died. Hypothetically, you could have just witnessed my drowning. Both of you. You're really hypothetical, Coolberg. I've noticed that."

"But we're *students*. With students, everything is hypothetical. Besides, we didn't witness your drowning. We tried to—" Theresa begins.

"And if you had seen me go," Nathaniel continues, "if I had disappeared, what then?"

"Oh, that's easy," Coolberg says from the backseat. "If we had seen you go, we would have been very sad. We would have presented the world with the grim face of tragedy." His elegiac tone of voice seems distant, avuncular, ironic.

"Sad? Jesus. That's not much," Nathaniel says. They drive for another ten minutes until they enter the outskirts of Buffalo. As if he had been thinking about word choices all that time, Nathaniel says, finally, "'Sad' isn't much of any-thing. I hate that word."

"But there's more," Coolberg continues. "I wasn't finished. You should let me finish. If you had disappeared, if you had died, we would have . . . we would have *become* you. We would have taken you on. We would have *turned into you*." He waits. "*You would have lived in us.*"

"I don't know what you're talking about," Nathaniel says. "Theresa, do you know what he's talking about?" Theresa shakes her head. "See? Theresa doesn't know either."

"When a person dies," Coolberg says, "the survivors take on the features of the deceased. The most eccentric traits are acquired first—tics, stuttering, shakes of the head. That's how grieving works. The living reimagine themselves as the one who has gone missing. I would have taken you over. That's what we would have done. I guarantee it."

"Speak for yourself," Theresa says.

"Oh, I never do that." Coolberg laughs.

14

FOR THE NEXT TWO MONTHS, as Buffalo descends into winter, Nathaniel often finds himself in one of two sets of arms: Theresa's or Jamie's. He does not, for now, think of himself as a hypocrite or a two-timer.

His love for Theresa happens to be contaminated by his doubts about her vaguely empty character. Still, he can't resist her nervous wit, or her catlike purring when they make love, or the sheer force of her physical attractions— her narrow waist, her perfect breasts, the knowing smile. As for Jamie, he has never been involved with a lesbian cab-driver before. Who has? The relationship, such as it is, follows no logic. The outcome is predictable. The situation bubbles on its surface with a comic pathos they both recognize: *Please kiss me* typically followed by *Do I have to?* Well, all women feign indifference, he believes. That's their scene. Courtly love requires that men must be educated through rejection, patience, and gift-giving.

Jamie's physical apathy toward Nathaniel gives her a certain distance about his needs, all needs, the human comedy of neediness, including her own. Indifference to him makes her into a wise guy. She is unsullied by any desire for him, and yet . . . With her, there are always those ellipses.

Standing on a kitchen stool near her refrigerator, replacing a bulb in the overhead fixture, he tells her, "Uh, you know, Jamie, I'm kind of falling in love with you. I've been dreaming about you lately."

"Oh," she says, "you are? You have been? And . . . where did that come from? That's an odd . . ." She tilts her head at him in silent inquiry.

"Yeah, I know," he tells her, screwing in the bulb and flinching when it suddenly goes on.

"Because . . . well . . . this is awkward," she says, "and . . . um, impossible, though not . . . heartrending yet . . . but . . . yes, certainly impossible . . ."

All the ellipses, the negative space around her responses to him—how could he not notice them? He lowers himself to where she has placed herself, near him. She touches him tenderly on the shoulder in thanks.

"I thought I would break my neck," he tells her. "If I fell off that stool, I mean."

Because what else is happening is that on certain other evenings when he lies on the floor of her little studio, surrounded by molded geometrical objects she has fished out of junkyards and altered and made beautiful with her blowtorch, he gazes up at the quasi cylinders, metal Möbius strips, and Styrofoam tetrahedrons hanging by wires and string from the ceiling, and he finds himself aroused and shaken by her talent, her vision of airworthy topological surfaces. Surely, somewhere in the United States another cabdriver is making skeletal flying machines out of Styrofoam and discarded plastic and junked metal, but he doesn't know where. Only here, on the Niagara Frontier, is such a gifted woman perfecting her art.

So out of masculine dutifulness and the tribute that love pays to accomplishment, he cooks dinner for her, elaborate three-course concoctions. He prepares the meals like a servant, a slave to love; he does not eat much himself, being enamored. A man in love cannot eat, keyed up as he is for a long journey. He listens to her disquisitions about the soul of materials, the mysteries of negative space, the genius of Giacometti and of David Smith, and the plotlessness of her interestingly fucked-up life, a life she claims she would not trade for anyone else's. In return, she lets him hold her in preprogrammed ways on certain predetermined nights, and on occasion she takes pity on his luckless erections. Is she beautiful? He hasn't always paid attention to that; her physical appearance seems irrelevant to his infatuation.

If she loved him the way a woman loves a man, she'd be jealous of Theresa. Or so Nathaniel likes to think. What interests her more (she claims) is Nathaniel's futile love for a lesbian sculptor, herself, and his nonsensical love for a blandly intelligent Marxist would-be academic and ironist. These are bad options. She remains intrigued by his waffling, his male duplicity. He is a case study in the problem of the masculine. For the time being, she has suspended her interest in other women, so that she can observe him unimpeded. She asks to hear what Theresa is like in bed, and when he starts to inform her, she abruptly refuses to hear the details. Sex between him and Theresa empties their souls of content, so she claims. Surely he can't be considering a vanilla life with such a trifling female, this . . . cipher.

Nathaniel lies on Jamie's mattress on the floor, watching her as she works. Clad in overalls, she taps and hammers away at the head of a small metallic bird. She applies percussive techniques at the workbench and then seems ready to use her fiery equipment to weld another wing onto the bird's torso until she decides that two wings are probably enough. On other evenings she assembles and disassembles rhombic dodecahedrons, meditating aloud on their shape, humming along to the radio or keeping up a monologue on arcane geometrical matters. Did Nathaniel know that Alexander Graham Bell, of telephone fame, once designed an elaborate flying contraption built out of small tetrahedron cells? No, he didn't. Or that Bell invented a man-lifting kite, the ancestor of parasailing devices? No.

She keeps up three or four projects at once. Dinners prepared by Nathaniel bake in the oven as she turns her brooding attention to a football-shaped piece of metal, perhaps a blimp or dirigible of some kind, meant to hang somehow in the air. Music from the radio: Bartók's second string quartet—clangorous Magyar scraping and sawing, *sul ponticello* wiry screeching, a Mitteleuropean racket perfect for a sculptor's studio—snarls its way out of the speakers into the air, keeping the blimp suspended. Around seven on the nights he is permitted to stay, they eat dinner, and one particular evening over lamb chops he asks her why she's a Roman Catholic.

"Oh, that? I'm sick in love with the Virgin Mary," she says unsmilingly. "She's my girl. I've been in love with her since I was ten years old. She came to me in a dream and said my name out loud. She's not an idea. She's real. I saw her face on the wall inside a movie theater, just before the lights went down. She exists. I've danced for her. She's a fact in my life."

"A movie theater. Like Max Jacob."

"Who?"

"Max Jacob. He was a French poet, pre–World War II. Jewish. He saw the face of Jesus on the wall of a movie the-

ater, and when it happened a second time, he went to the
Fathers of Zion, an order dedicated to converting the Jews.
At his baptism, Picasso served as his godfather."

After dinner, he washes up, reads, and she takes a long bath
in the claw-footed bathtub before she goes out to drive for
Queen City Cab. On those nights when she isn't working,
she emerges from the bathroom wrapped in a towel, and she
lies down with him on the mattress where he has been reading Norman O. Brown's *Love's Body*, a book whose ecstasies
already seem dated and stale. Tonight, he puts the book
aside. Together, naked under a comforter, they gaze up at
the ceiling from which are suspended Jamie's birds and
blimps. Above the art and to the side, a ceiling fan rotates
languidly.

"You know," she says, "you're kind of sweet, but I'll never
know why I got involved with you."

"Because you thought I deserved it. You said so. You initi-
ated this. Anyway, it's not really involvement."

"Oh, really? I *have* sucked your dick. That's intimacy, isn't
it? Still, I guess you're right. And I suppose I *did* start this,
didn't I? That'll teach me. Why did I do that?" She drapes
her left leg over him. Her thigh has a dancer's taut muscular
symmetry. "But you're a delay. You're just a man. You're
temporary." She smiles at the ceiling. "You understand me.
That's the danger part. It's like I'm Nixon, and you're my
Haldeman."

"Don't think so. You're not Nixon. No woman can be
Nixon. Not possible. He's one of us."

"Okay okay. But you know me and the sum of me and you
seem to know what I want," she says in a friendly growl.
"You're the first guy I've ever known who did. It's unfair."

"That's right. I do know. You want to fly away."

"Right. And I want another girl," she says, "to fly away with me. Not you. I can't fly away anywhere with you. With you, I'm grounded. Men are beasts of the ground."

"Uh . . . you sure about that?"

"Absolutely. You're all creatures of the mud. You can't help it. I know this feels weird. That desire I'm supposed to have for you? I don't have it. I sometimes wish it were there, but it isn't." She waits. "I sort of love you anyway, but a girl can't go on doing charity work for a mud-beast forever."

"See, the thing is," he says, "you can treat me as hypothetical. That's an adjective that guy Coolberg uses with me. Hypothetical this and hypothetical that. You haven't met him, but—"

"Oh, yes, I have," Jamie announces, her hand drifting down his chest. "He came a few days ago to the People's Kitchen and struck up a conversation with me."

"This was when?" Nathaniel has a sudden flushed sensation.

"Last week, I think. He asked me about working there, like he was planning on joining the collective. I couldn't remember seeing him before. He's friends with your other girlfriend, right? The real one? The one you're cheating on, with me? Theresa? The straight girl with the great tits, the high IQ, and the ironic knowing smile?" There's an accusatory pause. "Anyway, he asked me all sorts of questions about me. And you. Funny that I forgot to mention that I saw him. He seemed to know that you and I had this . . . well, I don't know, okay, this *hypothetical* thing going. He was curious about everything. He's a collector of facts, I guess. And so he told me a little bit about himself."

"What did he say?"

"Oh, you know."

"Actually, no, I don't."

"Well, he said he grew up in Milwaukee, until his family moved to New York, an apartment on West End Avenue. Didn't *you* live in Milwaukee, too? And New York? That's quite a coincidence. Anyway, he said he has a sister who was in a car accident and is mute. That's a shame—I felt bad for him. He said his father died when he was quite young, of a stroke—"

Nathaniel sits up quickly. He feels cold sweat breaking out on his forehead, and his chest heats up. "Wait! What? He said what?"

"You heard me." She looks over at him. "What's the matter?"

For a brief moment, Nathaniel looks down at his shape under the comforter, as if some part of him is no longer there. Where his right foot should be, nothing. Quickly he scrambles out of bed and rushes into Jamie's bathroom. His stomach has been seized with a sudden twist of electric current. He is afraid that he may be having a heart attack. A metaphysical nausea instantly converts itself into physical nausea, and he leans over the toilet bowl, staring downward. The seizure feels like a heart attack located in his gut. Maybe, he thinks, a heart attack can strike anywhere in the body. You could have a heart attack in your brain.

Jamie appears in the bathroom doorway, as naked as he is. In the midst of his nausea, he admires her legs. They are solid; they will not disappear on her. They will continue to hold her up, and maybe she will hold *him* up. "Nathaniel," she says, "what's going on?" She approaches him and puts her arm around him as if to support him, to keep him from falling.

He glances down to see if his right foot still exists. It does. It has returned. This is crazy, he thinks.

"That's not his life," Nathaniel says. Anger arrives belatedly. "The stroke, the mute sister, Milwaukee, New York—that's all mine. That's not his. It's *my* life."

"He's claiming your life?" Jamie asks. "That's preposterous."

"Okay, yeah, I know. But that's what he's doing."

"Are you feeling sick? Are you okay?" In the mirror's reflection, Jamie's face shows high-level concern, her dazzling eyes signaling that she's at home and the lights burn brightly. At this moment, when Nathaniel sees her face reversed in the mirror, he thinks that Jamie is the most beautiful woman he has ever looked upon, even though she is not beautiful. He is having another Gertrude Stein moment. *She is beautiful although she is not beautiful.*

"I have to go," Nathaniel tells her. On her bathroom mirror she has stuck a little decal that says WATERFOUL OBSERVATION SITE. In the bathtub is her collection of yellow rubber ducks and ducklings and orange shampoo bottles. The bathroom smells of primal girl. One of her metal dirigibles hangs from the bathroom ceiling. Jamie's little tchotchkes constitute a conspiracy of the hapless and lovable and airborne.

"Can't this wait?"

"I mean, it won't. No, it can't wait," he says, his verbal confusion adding to his rage. Something must be done. He feels like pulling down a few window shades and tearing them into small bitter pieces.

"Why did he do all that? Why does he want your life? Is he in love with you?"

Nathaniel says nothing.

"I bet he's in love with you." She stands behind him and reaches around him to lean her head against his shoulders. "I'm sort of worried about you." She waits while

Nathaniel notices that "sort of"—must everything she does be qualified?—and she touches him on the chest. "You're not going to hurt him, are you?" Little whiffs of physical desire are making their way from her toward him, little fugitive hetero longings. In the mirror, her eyes bore into him and her brow is furrowed. Maybe his current psychic crisis energizes her. His sudden suffering makes her want to bed him down. But it's his suffering she wants to have, to lay her hands on, not him.

"Oh, Jamie, not now," he says. He turns around and kisses her, then breaks the embrace to put his clothes on.

The metallic bird hanging to the side of the door sways back and forth, given life by his rushed departure.

15

No one answers at the Coolberg residence. Nor does he respond to pressed call buttons in the apartment building where, numerous times, Nathaniel has dropped him off. On the callboard are six names:

> Wendego
> Highsmith
> Augenblick
> H. Jones
> Bürger-Wilson
> Golyadkin

In Nathaniel's current state, they all feel like bogus names invented by a mad postmaster. No Coolberg here. Is there a Coolberg anywhere? The name itself sounds fictional and implausible, a poor effort at whimsy.

He calls Coolberg's number all night. No one answers.

At home the next morning, he stares at the telephone before calling his stepfather at his New York office on Water Street, near the East River with a view of the Brooklyn Bridge. On warm days when the wind is right, his stepfather claims, he can get a whiff of the Fulton Fish Market. Nathaniel hates to disturb him, but he needs some advice from a fully qualified adult. His stepfather is a "semi-pro capitalist," as he calls himself. An investor in start-up companies, he's an easygoing, charming moneymaker unafflicted by true greed. He doesn't mind being disturbed at work. He's placid and detached, observing with disinterested attention the tidal flow of capital. All he wants is to get his hands in that water from time to time and scoop out a few cupfuls of cash. The system continues to function thanks to coolheaded minor players like him. The raptors come and go on huge reptilian wings. Nothing surprises this man; nothing shocks him. His worldliness is a perpetual relief from everyone else's naïveté.

After chatting for a minute or so, his stepfather says, "So. Buddy boy. Something on your mind?" Nathaniel tells him that he has a problem. "Tell me," his stepfather says quietly, and Nathaniel hears an audible creak as his stepfather leans back in his leather chair. All successful middle-aged males love to listen to stories and to give advice, Nathaniel has noticed. They feel that mere survival has given them the right to pontificate. It's the Polonius syndrome; they all have it. But this one, this man, adores narratives; he is, by nature, an anecdotalist.

Nathaniel explains the intricacies concerning Coolberg to his stepfather, presenting the story as straightforwardly as possible. When he is finished, his stepfather clears his throat. He is going to respond to Nathaniel's story with another story. It is his way.

During his junior year in college in Maine, his stepfather says, a particularly bad winter dropped itself down over the community: colossal snows, day after day of subzero temperatures, radiators clanking all day, students coughing and getting frostbite and pneumonia. "Imagine the silences. Everything muffled. You couldn't even see outside," he says. "The frost and snow blocked the windows." No one could go anywhere. No one wanted to risk driving off the roads into a slow demise from disorientation and hypothermia. The roads were more or less impassable, but because most of the college faculty lived nearby, classes went on as scheduled. The sidewalks had snow piled on either side as high as your head—it was like walking through a tunnel just to get to calculus class. Old men died shoveling out their driveways. Their wives began talking to their cats on a daily, hourly basis. People had the feeling that the snows would never stop, that the flakes would continue to drift downward forever, lazily and implacably covering everything in a terrible white stupor.

"An old-fashioned winter. So we all burrowed in and found various occupations." The college bookworms curled up with their books; the basketball players played endless rounds in the gym; the lovers stayed in their beds, making love nonstop in the hope of reviving spring. Some slept together naked *with their doors open,* on display—modesty, for some reason, having abandoned them, the terrible privacy of a perpetual snowstorm calling forth its opposite, prideful noisy exhibitionism and shamelessness more often associated with the exposed skin of the tropics than with New England. Such cohabitation wasn't allowed in those days, but all the rules were being ignored. But for everyone else, those not completely erased by studiousness or by the fortunes visited by love, the snows became a spiritual and psychological problem—how to be distracted from the maddening iron chill, the accumulating white silences falling out of the sky?

Somehow, an idea was born, no one knew from where, one of those ideas that arises like bacteria spreading overnight in spoiled food. A bunch of guys formed a social club, the Merry Andrews. Six of them at first, then a dozen, then more, including a few women. They met surreptitiously. They called each other "Andrew"; everybody was an Andrew. Everybody dressed in identical clothing as the snows fell hour by hour outside. Women became Andrews and were invited into the drunken meetings filled with absurdist bureaucratic business about whom to admit and what protocols to follow. "Hello, Andrew," they said to each other. They affected the same speech patterns, they acquired identical tics during their encounters—the parties began in the afternoons and went through the nights into the following days until the beer and cigarettes inevitably ran out, when they would discuss the future: the future generally, and the future of the Andrews, and where to obtain more beer, more Scotch, more cigarettes, more drugs. All the Andrews seemed to get drunk at about the same time, and they all seemed to share the same tastes in the same songs, which they sang or played repetitively on their phonographs. They disappeared into each other; they vanished into a collectivity. Then the phenomenon spread to the college at large, at a slightly higher voltage. For two weeks, all the undergraduates called themselves "Andrew" in this epidemic folly, and a general breakdown in morals followed, as Andrews mated with other Andrews. The snow had induced this. The Southerners lost their drawls, the Midwesterners their flat vowels—everyone began to speak alike, except for the athletes, and the lovers, and the bookworms, who paid no attention.

"Then what happened?" Nathaniel asks.

"Then the sun came out," his stepfather says, "and everything returned to normal. Individuals became themselves again."

Nathaniel does not believe this story, but he appreciates

his stepfather having taken the trouble to think it up and to tell it. The narrative seems like a mask covering over another actual story that his stepfather will never tell, so Nathaniel asks, "Did anyone kill anybody else?"

His stepfather, puzzled, says that of course no one killed anyone else. Why would he ask such a question? "Why do you ask? People like us don't kill each other," he says. "We don't do that. But, now that I think about it," he adds, as an afterthought, "two people, two of these Andrews, did try to kill themselves."

"Each other?"

"No, *themselves*," his stepfather insists. "You know, suicide." He waits. "But they didn't succeed." Then he says something that sounds like his verdict on this particular history. "You know, few people really want to become individuals," he says. "People claim that they do, but they don't. They want to retain the invisibility of childhood anonymity forever. But that's not possible except in a police state. In an ordinary life, you have to become yourself." He takes a deep breath. "So. Classes going well?"

"Oh, yeah, the classes are fine."

"Good. Your mother's good. She misses you. Your sister's all right, too."

That "all right" also has a touch of the disingenuous itself, Catherine's condition being timeless and unreconciled to reality. Having refused to give up her lifelong mourning, she lives outside of Milwaukee in a small group home with a view of Lake Michigan. There, minded by salaried employees, she passes a contemplative life colored by the narrow spectrum of apathy, except for episodes at the piano. She has been given antidepressants, sedatives, and stimulants, but still she does not speak. She reads, or seems to: she glares at the words and turns the pages with impatient finger flicks.

Occasionally she peeps and squeaks. But when she sits down at the keyboard, she plays with a rather frightening virtuosity, though without any recognizable human feeling—the music emerges from the instrument with the dead expressionism of a player piano switched on in an empty room. Catherine's face remains vacant no matter what musical notation passes in front of her or what her fingers find to do to occupy the time.

The subject of the job market removes Catherine from the conversation, and soon his stepfather tells Nathaniel that he has to go back to work. If this were a real crisis, the old man would stay on the line, but for him identity has nothing to do with money or with how the world actually works, and that is that.

"Thanks, Pop," Nathaniel says. He puts down the phone and looks around at the comfortable dinginess of his apartment, now, thanks to the absence of valuables, unburglarizable. Outside the window, a cardinal chirps frantically as if affrighted. Nathaniel would like to snap off his imagination and its multiple narratives, but it's stuck in the ON position, and if he didn't live in his imagination half the time, he wouldn't be himself, and he wouldn't be bothered by Coolberg. Maybe he wouldn't be bothered by anything, period. He would live on the Blessed Isles.

He leans forward to gaze out the window. He sees his own reflection in the glass. What good is an identity, anyway? his reflection asks him. For that matter, what good is a reflection? *I lived in Wisconsin before I lived in New York,* he tells the reflection, *these were my parents, I broke my arm when I was twelve and Brian Hennerley tackled me when we were playing touch football, I first kissed a girl when I was fourteen, I remember she was ticklish* . . . the rubble of the personal, the dust motes of the specific. Who cares who you are? the reflection asks, pointing at him. Every identity consists of a pile of moldering personal clichés given sentimental value by the fact that someone owns them. The fallacy of the unique! A rubbish heap of personal data, anybody's autobiography. You can't sell it or trade it. Besides, everyone has an autobiography, the principle of inflation thereby causing each one to be worthless.

Well, okay, the reflection admits, maybe some identities do shape up better than others thanks to the clothing of grace and good fortune. Of course, of course, of course, *of course.* Some identities are *significantly* richer than others, you'd have to be a fool to deny it. Better, more magnificent sins enacted on satin sheets in the penthouse, with music piped in through the floor grates along with the perfume, lend a certain robust glory to a man's memory trove. Whereas some existences are empty dry sockets giving off the radiation of pain, victimization, mere shadows on the wall, dim bulbs, lethal vicissitudes, black holes in space, gigantic gravitational vacuums piloted by hungry ghosts . . .

Nathaniel finds that he is sweating again as these gigantic formless concepts tumble out of the window glass's reflection into him, taking up mental occupancy. The unpleasantness of these ideas causes him to radiate a nervous malodorous sweat that he himself can smell and be offended by, and to remedy the smell of himself, he rushes to his closet to put on a clean shirt. He searches among the hangers and in the dresser drawers for the blue Brooks Brothers that his sister gave him, once upon a time, the one with thin rust-colored vertical stripes and a button-down collar, the shirt that always cheers him up, the wonder-working shirt. Wearing it makes him into a serious man, what they used to call a *man of parts.* Outside, snow has started to fall and is tapping against his bedroom's window glass. The cardinal is no longer chirping, his reflection has disappeared, and the shirt's not here—it has gone conspicuously missing. The dresser drawer advertises its own emptiness. And what about the white shirt his stepfather gave him, the one tailored in Italy, the elegant Fratelli Moda? What about that one? That one isn't here either.

Where did they go? Who would burglarize two shirts?

Where are my shirts?

16

AT ONE OF THE TABLES in the dining area of the People's Kitchen sits Ben the Burglar, alone, slurping his soup. He wears a red cap. He eats with his gloves on, spoon in his right hand, lit cigarette in his left. Today he sports a pair of old tortoiseshell glasses, a 1940s look, that of a chump in a downtown diner wearing a cheap disguise, behind which his junkie eyes peer at his fellow citizens. A bruise shines from the left side of his jaw. Deep film-noir shadows fall on him; blue smoke rises from his head. It is four o'clock in the afternoon, and Nathaniel sits down next to him uninvited.

"Whad I do this time?" Ben asks without looking up. He swallows, then takes a puff from the cigarette.

"I'm missing two shirts," Nathaniel says. "I think you know where they are."

"Would you let me finish?" Ben slows down the eating process, savoring each bite of potato, carrot, and stew meat. Why hasn't he taken off his gloves? He needs a gangster affectation.

"You broke into my place again. That was unfair."

"So?" Ben smiles. "You didn't mind when I did it before."
Confessions of misdeeds apparently emerge easily from this
hard-boiled guy. Like any tradesman, he takes pride in his
work and in a job successfully accomplished. He smiles
coldly, blowing smoke upward toward the ceiling. It is an era
when people still know how to smoke and eat at the same
time.

"So why did you take those shirts?"

"You forgot to lock the door again, for starters. I took a
pair of pants, too," Ben says thoughtfully. "And a pair of
shoes."

He's now madly grinning with self-love. Also, his speech
has slowed down, an effect caused by the good life of cigarettes, food, and opiates. For him, heroin is to experience
what salt is to rice. It makes it palatable.

"How come you took them?"

"*How come?* I was on commission."

"You were *what?*"

"You're funny when you pretend to be deaf." Ben gazes up
at the ceiling with merriment. His eyes mist over. Life is one
long spree. He taps out ash on the coffee cup's saucer, then
rotates the cigarette's tip on the china, a delicate gesture
suitable for a dollhouse.

"On commission from whom?"

"'Whom.' I like that." He shakes his head in admiration.
"You sure got yourself a good education somewhere."

"Oh, fuck you, Ben."

"Okay, there you go, fuck me," Ben replies, rubbing his
chin violently before lifting his eyebrows to express radical
innocence in the line of questioning from this overeducated
spoilsport. After taking one last long drag from his cigarette,
he stubs it out on the saucer and exhales smoke through his
teeth. He resumes foraging in the bottomless bowl of soup,

prolonging the moment to excruciation, a delay that evidently delights him, because he smirks. Now, with his left gloved hand, free of the cigarette, he lifts a piece of bread, taking a delicate bite. The bread has been slathered with butter, and butter affixes itself to his chin, giving him the look of a polished wooden marionette.

"Coolberg. It was Coolberg, right? He found you."

The burglar shrugs. "A man's gotta eat."

"Which you're doing. For free. It's not as if you're dining off your ill-gotten gains."

"That's right. I gave the ill-gotten gains to Luceel. My *wife*. You remember her. You let yourself meet her, which she didn't want to do, with you. She didn't like your *looks*. She didn't want to make your acquaintance. Listen, I tell you what." Ben straightens up. His comic momentum appears to have diminished. "So here I am, okay, right? Eating?" He talks and chews with his mouth open, exposing his nutrition. "So. Okay. So look around at my kingdom."

Nathaniel involuntarily takes in the People's Kitchen. Its sights and smells—the graying dust on the front windows, the vinegary odor of cooked food and gamy dirty clothing, the collection of cast-off benches and chairs on which the four other shabby diners sit, absorbing what nourishment they can, the cars on Allen Street rumbling by in a gray audible haze—the entire scene, he knows, should depress him with its overtones of despondency, what his stepfather used to refer to, smilingly, as *miserabilium*. Gray day, grayer mood. But no: he feels comforted and slightly elated to be here among scruffy outcasts. These are his people.

"So what's your point?" Nathaniel asks.

"My point? My point? Listen, there's gotta be a word for people like you, people who get off being around people like me. I'm just trying not to go down the drain here, man.

Maybe you haven't noticed: my future ain't what it used to be."

He rubs at his chin. He is working himself up and shivers with agitation.

"You look at me. Okay, I got a habit. Also I got a pregnant wife, but we love each other, me and Luceel, and you come in here, asking me questions like I'm some award you got in the Good Deed Department. You sit there, college boy, pretending like I got a whole bunch of choices in life, a cookie jar full of cookies. You got a word for yourself, for what you are, you little shit, you slimeball educated fuck?" He says this quietly, with scary neutrality.

"A sentimentalist," Nathaniel says. "But I thought we were talking about my stolen shirts."

"Whatever." Ben takes another bite of bread. Outside a siren passes. "So, on account of you once made me a cup of coffee, I'll say this to you, at least: No, it wasn't whoever you said it was, Iceberg or Coolberg or Kustard or whatever the fuck his name is or was, who asked me for a couple of your shirts and the other stuff. Hey, someone comes up to me, askin' for help on a job, offering money, I don't ask this jerkoff who they are and what they want this shit for. I just do it."

"So who was it? Who was he?"

"Not a 'he.' It was a her. Your girlfriend."

"Jamie? What would Jamie want with my clothes?"

"That's funny. *You're* funny. Jamie. I like that. Me, I do my women one at a time. Sorry to disappoint you. I never heard of this Jamie. Wasn't her."

"Theresa?"

"That's the one."

"How'd she find you?"

"Guess you must've told her about me."

"Did she talk to you here?"

Ben shakes his head emphatically. "We're finished, you and me. No more questions, and no more answers neither." Ben takes his spoon and taps it twice on the soup bowl. "No, wait a minute, I just thought of something." He turns to gaze through his film-noir eyeglasses at Nathaniel for a long moment, during which the sounding clatter of dishware comes out of the kitchen, and Ben takes a stagy cigarette from his shirt pocket, sticks it into his mouth, and lights it with a safety match. Outside on the street, a car hoots. "You know what? I'm better than you." He inhales and nods, agreeing with himself. "Much better. I love my wife, is the thing. I don't have to apologize about that to no one. Okay, I'm a big screw-up. I'm a flop as a moneymaker. Mistakes were made. But I'm okay with that. You could even say I was happy, once I was dead." He points the cigarette at Nathaniel, and Nathaniel flinches. "And you are whatever you are."

17

HIDEOUSLY PERKY and upbeat, Theresa on the phone informs Nathaniel that, yes, indeed, she will certainly discuss the theft of his clothing (a joke! for heaven's sake! a *joke!*), but, no, she will not do so at his apartment or at hers, which she refers to as "*ma maison,*" the sexy irony in her voice side by side with comic pretentiousness. Then she coughs and says, "We're certainly *not* going to have a 'long serious talk,' as you call it, while we're sitting around somewhere. I don't like sedentary quarrels." Instead, they will meet at Delaware Park at the west end of the pond, and together they will jog until they reach the zoo, whereupon they will greet the lions and tigers and bears in the name of humanity before turning around and jogging back. Recriminations, she says with her customary cheerful detachment, are staged more effectively while doing something else, such as exercising or monitoring wild animals. He offers to pick her up, but she says that she will walk over to the park from Hertel Avenue by herself, as a warm-up.

Halfway there, adjusting the volume control on the VW's staticky inadequate radio while gazing out at the block south of the Central Park Grill, Nathaniel notices a man walking his dog, a huge mottled mongrel probably acquired at the pound. The dog pulls the man forward at the end of his—the dog's—leash, the man himself in the forward-tipping posture of a pre-topple, and just when the man does in fact lose his balance and Nathaniel simultaneously finds a good strong radio signal, he has one of those crippling thoughts that occasionally come into the mind unimpeded: Theresa is of course Coolberg's lover. She plays the chords of betrayal every day as a lark, monogamy being a hilariously bourgeois bad habit, as is, or was, the story of her ex, Robby the Robot who resides in Berkeley, and furthermore, if he—Nathaniel—actually loved her instead of just thinking that he did, he would have already called her by now. He would have called her immediately. He would have confided in her, man to woman, lover to lover, as soon as he had found out from Jamie, who (the epiphanies will not stop) is the woman he actually loves, that Coolberg was clothed in his—Nathaniel's—autobiography. And now his actual clothes.

The pronouns are getting horribly mixed up. His, hers.

I am sometimes oblivious but seldom obtuse. Now I am both.

Maybe I am not actually here anymore.

18

IN THE PRECISE SPOT where she had said she would be, Theresa, wearing warm-up garb, stands stretching and flexing, and when she catches sight of Nathaniel, she smiles. It's tough to carry through on a grudge against an attractive insincere woman when she smiles at you that way. The smile is like an irresistible cheap song. Nathaniel smiles back. He can't help himself. No wonder they call what she has a *winning* smile. She wins. She always wins. Her hair's held back in that same ponytail she had displayed when he first met her, and now she leans over to limber up, placing her hands almost flat on the ground, and when she straightens, she takes him in her arms quickly and kisses him in a perfunctory good-morning way.

"April fool," she says.

"It's still November."

"You're so serious," she announces, tapping his chest. "And literal. You're *earnest*. I don't like that part of you. Well, are you ready to run?"

He nods. She takes off her sweatpants and trots over to Nathaniel's car, which she evidently knows is always

unlocked on principle (another one of Nathaniel's prin-
ciples, like the nonexistence of a watch on his wrist), and
drops them in.

Before he has been able to stretch or loosen up, she takes
off. Theresa has gained the distance of a city block when he
finally catches her. He's reasonably fit and manages to overtake her without too much trouble, but when they reach a
jogging path, she sprints ahead of him.

"So what's your question?" she asks him, throwing the
words to him, backwards, behind her.

"Those shirts?" he asks. "That burglar?"

"Him? Ben? You introduced us, remember?" Nathaniel
remembers no such thing. "Anyway, I wanted to wear one of
your shirts, to have you close to me. Really, Nathaniel, I do
have moments like that."

Nathaniel jogs around a hissing overfed goose, which
lunges at him, and he tries to coordinate his pace with
Theresa's. But she has a habit of changing her speed whenever he's next to her. A bird seems to be flying alongside
him, and one of his familiars, a bag lady with a Band-Aid on
her forehead caked with dried blood, stares at him fixedly
from a bench. He runs off to the side to make way for
another jogger, and when he does, Theresa slows down.

"I don't think I believe you. I think you gave my clothes
to Coolberg."

"Why would I do that?" She falls in behind him. "Well,
maybe I *did* do that."

"Are you seeing him?" he asks, throwing off the words to
the wind.

She says something that sounds like "*Seeing* him? Of
course I'm seeing him," and Nathaniel would feign surprise
and stop dead in his tracks, but he can't pretend to be
shocked—it would be insincere shock—and besides, he's in

no position to complain to her about anyone's sexual duplicity. He's not angry because he's not jealous because he
doesn't love her. Also, she can't see the expression on his
face, so why bother? "And you," she seems to say, from
behind him. "You're balling that dancer, that cabdriver."

"How do you know?" he asks the wind.

"I followed you once," the wind says to him, without
inflection. "I looked in through the window at you two. She
was performing for you. Scarves and shit. Very Isadora
Duncan."

This seems possible, so he drops the subject. Why isn't *she*
angry, if she took the trouble to be a voyeur? Maybe she just
has a little curiosity about him, a shallow blank desire that
lighted on him before it found its way into another corner,
to another object, a suitable target for her brand of erotic
whimsy. She is a kind of avant-garde lover, the type who will
try anything without being truly invested in it. Voyeurism
suits her perfectly; from where she watches, she occupies a
zone of safety.

"Is Coolberg wearing my clothes right now?"

"Could be. He's writing a story. He needs to be you for a
while."

"Oh, no." He feels as if he's been kicked in the stomach.
He struggles for breath as he runs. At last he manages a
question. "What's the story about?"

Theresa catches up to him, jogs alongside him for a
minute, then accelerates. Ahead of him, tossing up mud and
dirt from her running shoes, she says, "He's writing a book
called *Shadow*." She's panting slightly now from her exertions. "The first part is about a solar eclipse. The second sec-
tion is set around the time of World War I and is about
someone named Pierre Chadeau who's followed around by
his cousin, Henri l'Ombre, a ghost, who died on the front in

Belgium. The third part takes place entirely at night. That's the one with you in it."

"What role do I play? What do I do?"

She slows down again, turning around, jogging backwards, facing him. She seems to have no fear of stumbling or running blindly, backwards, into anything. She raises her hands to her forehead and sticks her index fingers out toward him, as horns. "You're the devil," she says, grinning.

19

THE ZOO SHOULD HAVE BEEN loud and smelly, with children milling around taunting the big cats for having been caught and caged, their kiddie-mockery accompanied by peanut shells launched toward the bars, and contemptuous laughter hurled at the now harmless teeth, the useless claws. There should have been trumpeting by unhappy elephants, desperate despairing silent roars sent up into the air by the voiceless imprisoned zebras, and there should have been peacock-shrieking.

But sometimes it happens that we enter a public place and find that, for once, the law of averages has broken down. We step gingerly into the darkened movie theater; the film starts, and we are the only ones in attendance, the only spectators to laugh or scream or yawn in the otherwise empty and silent rows of seats. We drive for miles and see no one coming in the other direction, the road for once being ours alone. Our high beams stay on. *Where is everybody?* The earth has been emptied except for us as we make our stuttering progress through the dark. We take each turn expecting that someone will appear out of nowhere to keep us company for a moment. In the doctor's anteroom, no one else is waiting and fidgeting with nerves, and the receptionist has vanished; or we find ourselves alone in the fun-house at the seedy carnival, where, because of our solitude, there will be no fun no matter what we do; or we enter the restaurant where no one else is dining, though the candles have all been lit and the place settings have been nicely arranged. The waitstaff has collectively decamped to some other bistro even though they have left the lights on in this one. The water boiling in the kitchen sends up a cloud of steam. The maître d' has abandoned his station; we can sit anywhere we please. The outward-bound commuter train starts, but no one else sits in the car, and no conductor ambles down the aisle to punch a hole in our ticket. In the drugstore no one is behind the cash register, and the druggist has left the prescription medications unmonitored on their assorted shelves. We enter the church for the funeral, and we are the first to arrive, and we must sit without the help of the ushers. Where are they? No sound, not a single note or a chord or a melody line from the organ loft, consoles and sustains us.

Such occasions are so rare that when they occur, we often think *I don't belong here, something is wrong* or *Why didn't they inform me?* or *Let there be someone, anyone, else.* But for the duration, when the law of averages no longer applies, we are the sole survivors, the only audience for what reality wishes to show us. This may be what the prophets once felt, this ultimate final aloneness.

So it was for Nathaniel and Theresa entering the Buffalo Zoo. "It looks like the maintenance hour," she says, briefly jogging in place. "Nobody's here."

"Nobody's here," Nathaniel says, repeating her phrase, stating the obvious out of sheer surprise.

"And the cages are empty," she says, pointing. Before

them is a large zoological space defined by bars in front and walls on the side, and a small landscape near the back with a water trough, on which float a few haystraws. Where is the rightful inhabitant, the animal?

"Isn't there a sign for what's supposed to be in there?" he asks.

She looks up. "No." She turns and with a thin smile seems about to say something. Then she touches her finger to her mouth and shakes her head twice. How complicated, and yet how simple, her inner dialogues must be.

Nathaniel pivots away from her and walks in a northward direction. Here are other cages, a few with identifying labels, and although some animals are on display, they are, one and all, sleeping. Here is Mika the Tiger, stretched out, eyes closed, possibly tranquilized. Over there is Gottfried the Panther—the name is affixed to the bars—also slumbering. Have all the animals here been given narcotics? He remembers a story about the Cumaen Sybil, who was granted a wish for eternal life but forgot to ask for eternal youth to accompany it, and who was immured in some sort of pen, where she grew older and older and smaller and smaller, until she was no larger than a spot of dust, crying out for death to deliver her.

Perhaps they have brought her here.

"I'm not a devil," Nathaniel says to Theresa.

"Well, it's his story," Theresa informs him, rubbing down her calves, "and he'll decide what you are. You present various temptations, don't you? In the meantime he's wearing your shirts and your shoes." She takes his hand. "I don't see why you have a problem with that."

"Ever heard of private property? Ever heard of theft? Besides, where has he been? I haven't seen him lately. It's as if he's been hiding," Nathaniel says, releasing her hand but keeping his eye on her legs, which are ostentatiously long and smooth-muscled. "He doesn't answer the phone and he doesn't seem to live in the building where I thought he lived."

"Nothing dates like the past," Theresa says with a slow drag on the word "past," as if this exposition were all old, tedious information with which she couldn't be bothered.

"Well, where is he, then?"

Theresa points. "Coolberg? He's right over there."

In the distance, through the pedestrian avenue between cages and the shuttered popcorn stand, is a bench on which Coolberg sits, facing them, one arm flung back. Theresa has conjured him out of nothing. When Nathaniel sees him, Coolberg raises his eyes from the book he's reading and meets Nathaniel's gaze, quizzically. The gaze turns into another stare. Some sort of telepathy has informed him that now is the moment for the exchange of glances. Under his unzipped jacket, the Brooks Brothers shirt he wears does not quite fit him, and the trousers need alteration, downward, about a half inch. The shoes appear to fit perfectly.

"You arranged this," Nathaniel says. "You planned this out and arranged this."

"Oh, no," she replies. "The totally empty zoo? An accident. The bored sleeping animals? A mere coincidence. Don't call me a bitch before you're ready to back it up."

"I never called you a bitch. I never did that." The outside air has the enclosed noncirculatory staleness of a cedar closet, and Nathaniel feels his hands closing up into clenched fists. As he runs toward Coolberg, he hears Theresa say something whose exact words he can't make out. But the sentence sounds like "*Don't* hit him."

When he arrives in front of Coolberg, Nathaniel says, "Stand up."

"Hi, Nathaniel. Ever read this?" He holds up a book entitled *The Wandering Beggar.*

"No. Stand up."

"Why?" He seems puzzled. "I'm glad to see you."

"Stand up so I can slug you."

"What good would that do? If you hit me, nothing would really happen."

"Something would happen. I'd feel good."

"Oh, but you're not like a character in a movie. Why act like one? That's a movie line. You keep underestimating yourself. You make yourself into less than you are. Well, you can hit me if you really want to, I suppose. I suppose you have the moxie for it. And by the way, I'm going to return your clothes and this pair of shoes in a few days, you know. I was *always* going to return them. I just needed them for a while."

"Stand up."

"Don't be that way. Ah, here's Theresa." Coolberg does indeed stand up as Theresa joins them. She's humming "Here Comes the Sun" in a high cheerful soprano. For some reason, her hands are crossed over her breasts. Ignoring her, Nathaniel hauls back and swings his fist into Coolberg's stomach. But Coolberg is an unsatisfactory victim, and the sensation is oddly like punching a Bozo the Clown doll. Nathaniel's fist meets little or no resistance, as if the fogged-in body it struck had anticipated and already made a place for the fist, accommodating this and every other occasion of physically intrusive violence, with fog. Nevertheless, Coolberg gasps and falls back onto the bench. The strangest part of it is that Theresa does not stop humming the Beatles tune as she reaches around Nathaniel to keep him from swinging his fist again. But how would he hit a man sitting on a park bench anyway? One blow must suffice.

"Okay . . . now you've done that . . . sit down." Coolberg gasps.

After what seems to be a blank, a blackboard of empty space and time suddenly inscribed with a few chalky words of instruction that vanish as soon as they have appeared, Nathaniel finds himself sitting on the bench next to Coolberg. Despite his intention to leave these confounding people at the zoo and to drive home, here he is nevertheless, their straight man. Around Coolberg, good intentions have a negligible effect. Coolberg, the recipient of Nathaniel's sudden attack, appears to have resumed reading *The Wandering Beggar* and now obligingly begins a plot summary. In the meantime Theresa has maneuvered her body, and herself, behind the two men and has one hand on Coolberg's shoulder and another hand on Nathaniel's. Her puppeteer fingers—she wears bright maroon nail polish—have him in a controlling grip. They rise and begin to caress his neck.

I love these stories, Coolberg says. They're about the adventures of Simple Shmerel, who travels from village to village. It's almost like *The Arabian Nights*.

Theresa kneads Nathaniel's shoulder. Then her fingertips move up to his earlobes.

This story, the one I'm reading now, is about Calman, the rich merchant, and Zalman, his coachman.

"I'm leaving," Nathaniel says.

Zalman is a good coachman, honest and sober. He even goes to bed early. But he has a vice: he imitates his master. For instance, he walks with his hands clasped behind his back in a thoughtful posture, like Calman's own attitude and bearing when walking, and he imitates his master's tone of voice and uses many of the same words and expressions.

"Let go of me," Nathaniel says.

One day Zalman steals Calman's clothes and begins to

wear them. Now no one can tell Zalman and Calman apart, so alike do they appear. The two of them, master and man, are indistinguishable even to those who know them. Both have glossy black beards and brown eyes. Zalman begins to give orders to Calman, and Calman protests. He does not take orders! He himself is the merchant, Zalman the mere coachman! To no avail. Everything is upside down.

"I'm going," says Nathaniel.

At last Simple Shmerel is summoned by the befuddled villagers, who want everything to return to normal. Simple Shmerel considers the puzzling situation, then orders the two men into an adjacent room. After a moment, Simple Shmerel speaks up. "Servant, come here!" he says. Almost instantly, Zalman opens the door and pokes his head in.

"Yes, sir?" he asks.

"There's your Zalman," points out Simple Shmerel. Apparently the habits of servitude cannot be broken.

Coolberg closes his book.

"Fuck you," Nathaniel says.

"Obscenities again. So tiresome. Well, maybe," Coolberg mutters, in an apparent non sequitur. The two men rise from the bench simultaneously as if under orders. Nathaniel feels light-headed, as if he is going under: he is gradually succumbing to some general anesthesia set loose at the zoo, or perhaps a hypnotic spell has been cast upon him. He needs a good night's sleep. He hasn't rested well lately. As he and Coolberg walk across the park, Theresa following them, Coolberg begins to narrate another plot summary, this time of the book he is writing, the one that takes place entirely at night, the one with Nathaniel in it, called *Shadow.*

In the story a young man, a student, a somewhat fever-brained type, loves two women at the same time. One of these women is a brilliant student, a polyglot, and a reader of Sumerian sacred texts; the other is a painter. Women have always loved this young man; he is gracious to them, considerate and thoughtful, and besides, he is disconcertingly beautiful, athletic, with long blond hair that the women imagine being trailed languorously over their bare skin under the covers as he kisses them, over their breasts and thighs, that is, until the force of Eros flings the covers back. But the strain of loving two women is one that few men can withstand. Even Ezra Pound lost his mind by loving two women. This young man, this character named Ambrose, develops an antipathy to daylight because in his doubleness, his double-heartedness, he fears that he will meet himself on the sidewalk coming toward himself from the opposite direction. At the same time that he is developing a phobia to daylight and the solidity of actual things, he is also receiving phone calls from an ambiguous Iago-like character named Trautwein, who, through brilliance and charm, gradually convinces him that the second woman, the painter he loves, who suffers for her art in poverty, has been cheating on him. There will be an unspecified fire. A violent death is indicated. However, certain parts of the story have only been sketched out; possibilities have presented themselves but have not turned into probabilities, much less inevitabilities.

"That's crap," Nathaniel says. "Sumerian texts? Please." An implausible detail: it takes decades to learn how to read those texts. Nathaniel's knees are shaky. Drops of perspiration appear as if by magic on his forehead, and unbidden tears spurt into his eyes. What if something were to happen to Jamie? What if these two sociopaths enacted . . . one of their fictions on her?

"I've got to go," he says, taking off toward his car.

Behind him he hears Theresa shout, "My sweatpants. They're in your car!"

What is the expression? *Clothes make the man.*

"*I made you so beautiful,*" the wind says. "*And you didn't thank me.*"

20

JAMIE IS SLEEPING. She may even be sleeping with another woman. Anyway, she is not answering the phone.

Nathaniel waits for a day and then shows up on her doorstep, ringing ringing ringing the doorbell until she opens the door and says to him, "What happened to *you*? You've got bags under your eyes. Were you up all night? Well, come in."

She shepherds him into the tiny kitchen, takes off his jacket, which she hangs on a wall hook, and sits him down close to a little metallic duck standing guard on the counter. He tells her that he hasn't eaten today, he hasn't been able to eat at all, much less sleep, so she pours him a glass of milk and in silence makes him a quick cheese omelet, which he picks at.

"Your teeth are chattering, and you're not chewing," she says. "You're *trembling* the food up."

"Right. I know." His fork rattles against the dinnerware.

"What's going on? It's getting late. I have to go to work."

"It's never been later than it is now," he tells her. He reaches across the kitchenette table and takes her hand.

Jamie has a strong woman's hand, and he touches her fingers one by one, precious humanity, beloved warmth. "There's something I have to tell you," he says.

"What's that?"

"I love you." He squeezes her fingers. "I've been in a fever. I love you with all my heart. I know it's hopeless and crazy, but, uh, I have to say this right now, this minute, this second. I love you, and I've just realized it these last days, and everything else is irrelevant, and now I have to tell you. I can't eat. I can't sleep. I can't *think*."

"You do? You did?" There's no mistaking her surprise, but at least she doesn't indicate amusement at statements of helpless emotion. A practical woman, she takes his plate and begins to rinse it in the sink. "What do you mean, 'last days'?"

"What? Oh, Jamie." He likes saying her name, so he says it again. "Jamie. Sit down. Please. Forget about the dishes. Sit down."

"Okay."

"Dear," he says. "Darling." He's not used to talking like this. The language of love and endearment seems hopelessly outmoded to him. Using such idioms is like walking into a dusty Victorian bedroom where cheap chromos of nymphs and cupids hang on the wall. The side tables and overstuffed armchairs have been degraded from years of abuse. Still, it's all he has. If he doesn't say what's in his heart, he'll die.

"What's come over you?" she asks. She's wearing her usual work-at-home outfit: t-shirt, bib overalls, tennis shoes, and now a red flannel shirt on top of everything, for warmth in the underheated apartment. She has a few flecks of metal in her hair.

"I was up all night last night. I couldn't sleep. I can't stop thinking about you. This is really love. I'm sure of it now.

I've been doing inventories of you. I've done a checklist. I think about your sculpture, your dancing, your good heart. Your hands. Your eyes. Your hair. I think about you over at the People's Kitchen. I think about your soul. Your soul! Listen to me. But I can't help it. The more I think about you, the more . . . the more I hunger for you. I even love it that you're a lesbian."

"Jesus, Nathaniel."

"I know. I *know*. This is really uncool. But I want someone who's messed up the way you are, and your eyes, and your everything, I want it all. I know you don't think you're beautiful and maybe you're not, but *I* think you are. It's the way you talk when you're talking, and it's the little sculptures on your windowsills, and the fact that the world is okay because you're in it. It's everything about you. It's the way you smell. It's the odor of your soul."

"How's that?"

"You smell clean," he tells her. "Like the soap of heaven." He waits. Her hand in his hand has relaxed a bit, and he holds her palm over his so that he can caress her fingers. Even at this moment, making a complete fool of himself, he recognizes that this is really love, because he could caress her fingers forever. Time would cease. Nothing now, or ever, would present itself as what he would rather do than this.

"I don't know what to say," she tells him.

"I know that."

"I'm not pretty."

"I don't care," he announces proudly.

"I'm attracted to other girls," she insists. "Your father would spin in his grave if he saw me coming home with you."

"Oh, let him rotate," Nathaniel says, in a freeing rush. "Please, honey," he says, "don't ever let anything happen to you."

"I'm not planning on it," she laughs, pulling her hand away. He takes it again.

"This is desperation you're witnessing," he says, gripping her. All at once, the thought occurs to him that what he's expressing is not love but hysteria, rising out of his own emptiness. He is in the grip of inflated speech, exaggeration, all the insincere locutions of opacity and self-deception. He is becoming, he feels with sudden queasy recognition, like a character in a plot dreamed up by someone like Coolberg. Nevertheless, he goes on, believing that he can explain himself, as his language veers further out of his control, as if he were behind the wheel and the steering had failed in the car—a dirt road, a tree straight ahead of him, an accident resulting in the loss of speech. "I'm a desperate man," he says, the words coming out of his mouth unaccompanied by inflections. "Oh, I love you. I can't say it enough. My dear, you're the one." Appalled by himself, and triumphant, he waits for her response.

This time she does pull her hand away firmly. "No, Nathaniel," she says quietly. "Nathaniel, I am *not* the one. Listen to yourself."

"You are. You are, you are, you are."

Sometimes he was insisting what he was sure about and when he was sure about it, he could not stop himself from insisting because it was the thing that he was knowing and by knowing this thing he could be correctly insisting and not stopping what he was telling and saying and telling again and again and again by really knowing. Why did Gertrude Stein continue speaking to him? Why would she not leave him alone? She loved women, too; that was why. She understood.

"I'm not. Really I'm not, I'm not, I'm not. You're deluded. Listen: I *can't* love you the way you love me. A woman has to love a man all the way down to the root. Otherwise, it's the usual disaster. A true marriage exists between bodies and souls. And I can't— I can't love you that way. I like you. I even love you sometimes, for a man, for what you are. I gave you my bed to lie in and my body, too, because you deserved it. You needed a buddy in bed, and that was me. You're a good man, maybe the best I've known. But we just slept with each other and liked each other a lot, and that's not love. That's an arrangement." She waits. "Did that other girl give you an ultimatum?"

"People are after you," Nathaniel says to her.

"What?"

"People are after you. Those two, Coolberg and Theresa."

"They are not after me. She may be jealous, but that's her problem, not mine."

"No, I think they're really after you."

"Honey. Nathaniel. You are really messed up. You should get help."

"There's something I have to do," Nathaniel tells her. "I love you, Jamie, please, and I have to do this right now." More foolishness, maybe, but none of his actions are under his control. He stands up and takes her hand—she does not resist this time, as he thought she might—and he guides her into the bathroom. He sits her on the bathtub's edge, and he squats down to unlace her shoes, first the left, then the right. Kneeling before her, he takes her sneakers off. Jamie watches him quietly, unprotesting. He peels off her white socks, then grabs a washcloth.

"Oh, no," she says.

Quickly he dips the washcloth into a stream of warm water and begins to wash her feet. He can feel her resistance, as she tenses her muscles and tendons, before that tension gives way to the sheer force of her astonishment.

"What are you doing?"

He does not look up. "I love you," he says, keeping his

eyes down. Tears are rolling off his cheeks. He does not wipe them away. When his task is completed, he tosses the washcloth on the floor, like any ordinary man. Out of abjection and pure longing, he bows his head before her. He waits.

Jamie takes Nathaniel's face in her hands and lifts it so that she can look at him. "All right," she says, the tears coming into her own eyes, laughing, shaking her head. "All right," she tells him, "take me to bed. Make me late to work."

"That's not what I'm telling you. That's absolutely not what I'm asking for here."

"I know what you're asking for," Jamie says equitably. "But this is all you'll get."

Half an hour later, his eyes closed, then suddenly opened, tears and sweat dripping down onto her, he calls out her name, and in response Jamie comes at the same time that he does. Her facial expression is one of pleasure mixed with horrified surprise. After a moment—she has broken out into quick shocked laughter—he looks into her eyes and imagines that her spirit, without knowing how or why, has suddenly disobeyed the force of gravity that has governed it. Her soul, no longer a myth but now a fact, ascends above her body. Like a little metallic bird unused to flight, unsteady in its progress, her soul rises and falls, frightened by the heights and by what it sees, but excited, too, by being married to him for a few seconds, just before it plummets back to earth.

21

BACK IN HIS APARTMENT, more clothes seem to be missing, more objects burglarized. The Escher print has disappeared from the wall; the phone is gone. The notebook on the desk appears also to have been filched. You'd think someone would at least leave a thank-you note. Outside the window, down the block, an old woman wearing a grotesquely jaunty Easter bonnet keeps him under surveillance from behind her loaded-down grocery cart.

Nathaniel goes into his bedroom. It is dinnertime. The apartment is feasting on subtractions. In a few days they may take his name away along with his address. Who or what could possibly stop them? Still, he will fight them. A few objects still remain here, unstolen. A book on the bedspread, the *Brownstone Eclogues* of America's forgotten great poet, Conrad Aiken, whom even burglars don't want to read, remains open to the stanzas he had been studying the day before. The poems consist of complicated farewell gestures to vanishing elements of American life—including the ordinary virtues. These poems, the intruders haven't taken.

Perhaps they don't care for the art of verse. He gazes down at the closing lines from "The Census-Takers."

And we are the census-takers; the questions that ask
from corner and street, from lamp-post and sign and face;
The questions that later tonight will take you to task,
When you sit down alone, to think, in a lonely place.

Did you ever play blind-man's buff in the bat-flit light?
Stranger, whose heart did you break? and what else did you do?—
The census-takers are coming to ask you tonight;
The truth will be hurrying home, and it's time you knew.

Absolutely right. It's time you knew. The lines have the quick comic jokiness, the perky melodramatic intelligence, of everyday despair. Meanwhile, Nathaniel stands up, sits down, kneels. He reads while fidgeting. He can no longer sit still. A prayer is coming upon him. When the spirit of prayer arrives in the bat-flit light, he must give way to it.

There is no organized religion whose articles of faith Nathaniel believes in. So when he prays, he has nothing to go on. He lacks authority figures and trustworthy spiritual guides. He prays sitting down or standing up or lying flat on the floor with his face bordered by his outstretched arms like a penitent. In his private faith are several articles: Life is a gift and is holy. Love is sacred. Existence is simple in its demands: We must serve others with loving-kindness. Some entity beyond our knowing is out there. Nathaniel believes that this unknowable force is paying attention to him. He has no idea why. The God that watches and loves him cannot be a personal God. Also: Is God, as the theologians insist, perfect? Somehow he doubts it. But he feels as if he knows as much about God as an ant knows about the room into which it creeps and crawls. Which is to say that he acknowledges that he knows nothing about God.

So today, now, this evening, he puts down the book and lies on the floor, placing his forehead on the linoleum tile. His penis is still thick from his lovemaking with Jamie. His body, wracked with discomfort, spreads itself out flat. That is how it should be. The words travel up out of his mind into the great nothingness.

Thank you for my life, he thinks, *thank you forever and always. Thank you for the gift of this woman who is also holy and sacred to me. Thank you for the sight of her and for my joy in her company and for her moment of joy also with me. Thank you for my guardian, Gertrude Stein. Blessings upon all the poor and unfortunate. May they be given food and love as I have been given these gifts. Suffering is necessary, I know. I do not know why it is necessary but I know that it is. Blessings upon all children and all innocent creatures such as animals at the zoo. Blessings upon those who suffer. May their sufferings be relieved. Blessings upon my dear mother and my kindly stepfather and my poor sister. Why have I been called a devil? For myself I ask for very little. But I ask for your care for this woman I love, for Jamie Esterson, who has danced for you, and I ask that no harm come to her. May nothing harm her now, I beg of you.*

Then everything goes dark.

PART TWO

22

ALL THIS HAPPENED a long time ago.

These days I work in a local arts agency writing up grant proposals. Our office puts poets (and sometimes out-of-work actors and musicians and dancers) into the schools. I am rather good at the work I do and take some pride in it. I'm able to give a sense of urgency to the project descriptions. A certain studied eloquence is not beyond my reach. I have a good track record for landing foundation money. I can point to successes. People believe me.

For a brief period a few years ago I worked as an insurance adjuster but found the job distasteful—I had to go around discounting distress. My task was to soft-pedal the damages. After flooding, after windstorms, after fire, I showed up to say, "Well, *that's* not so bad." You can't do such work for very long without suffering the consequences. The victims of calamity end up despising you. Years before my days as an adjuster, I served as an assistant editor for a small-town newspaper—I did some copyediting and reporting and sold advertising space. Before that, I was assigned to the role of the seemingly amiable person at the other end of the line to whom you talk when you call to ask about your utility bill. Prior to my time at Amalgamated Gas and Electric, I made phone calls—very briefly—at a collection agency. Early in my life as a working man, I delivered the mail.

My jobs have not defined me. With a minimum of training, almost anyone could have had my employment record without leaving a trace.

I have become an altogether different person from the man I once was. Now I'm something, someone, else. You might not notice me. I am in disguise. Mine is an old story.

Keats describes his "knight-at-arms" who fell in love with a beautiful maid, *la belle dame sans merci,* as having awakened "on the cold hill's side." I woke up there, too, alone. Like Keats's knight, I was found "palely loitering"—beautiful phrase. Cold hill's side. Palely loitering.

23

BEING A PARENT to two sons involves complicated logistics. This is one of those clichés that happens to be true. You have to plan ahead to make sure the car has arrived in the correct place at the correct time. The scheduling of such matters may seem trivial, but family life cannot be managed otherwise. The weekly roster attached to the refrigerator dictates who should be where, and when. Without it, chaos would descend on all of us. Jeremy, our older boy, has to be picked up after swim practice at exactly six thirty p.m. most days. If I were to forget or slip up, he would feel demeaned and ignored. But I have never forgotten.

When I'm scheduled to get him, and my wife, Laura, stays at home to make dinner, I sit there waiting in the car facing the exit doors of the locker rooms. Outside, evening has come on, and darkness has descended, except for those scattered pools of illumination under the parking lot's floodlights. In cars near my own, other adults await their children, all of us clustered together in a parental flock. Some keep their motors running so that the warm interiors will seem comforting when their kids open the door. Certain parents—

I am one of them—think that this practice wastes gasoline and is ecologically unsound. My car will warm up fast enough once I have started the engine.

It is peaceful here. I keep the radio going, usually tuned to the public radio classical music station, sometimes to a local jazz station that is struggling to stay afloat. The afternoon programming director at the classical station likes the music of Hector Berlioz and often puts that composer's shorter pieces into the rotation. A few weeks ago, they were playing *Harold in Italy* while I watched the kids straggle out.

What's odd is that the girls always show up first. You'd think the boys would appear before the girls do, but, no, it's the girls who emerge initially, with their hair pulled back or scrunched up. They often stand there while their eyes get used to the semi-dark. They look exhausted. They scan the parking lot for their parents. (The rich kids scurry to their own vehicles and drive off, but ours is a public school in the suburbs, and there isn't that much flaunting of wealth.) The girls find where their moms or dads have parked, and they clamber in. The cars start up and drive away.

Then the boys wander out, many of them wearing earbuds connected to their iPods. Boys, I have noticed, listen to music much more often than girls do. Although they take longer to shower and dress (why? it is a great mystery), they have invariably failed to comb their hair. Their hair goes up and out every whichway. The boys' faces have that circle-around-the-eyes raccoon look from the swimming goggles they wear, and, also like the girls, they have the appearance of complete exhaustion.

If I am part of a car pool, Jeremy and one or two of his teammates will throw their backpacks in the trunk and drop themselves wordlessly onto the front or back seat. Instantly the car smells of chlorine. If Jeremy is alone, he tosses his gear on the floor and sits down next to me. I ask him how his day went, and he usually shrugs and says, "Okay." I have learned not to push a conversation on him. He's usually too tired to make a social effort anyway.

All he wants, most nights, is to get home so that he can eat dinner. His appetite seems to know no bounds; he's always famished.

You would think that in a car pool the boys would start talking to each other, but they don't. They just sit there, mute, waiting to be delivered. Sometimes a few syllables are muttered, a sentence fragment here or there: that's all. Tiny shards of music—death metal, hip-hop, rap, folk rock, whatever—fly around the car's interior from their earbuds.

On the night the radio station was playing *Harold in Italy,* I accidentally kept it on. Typically I turn the car's radio off when Jeremy gets in. I had forgotten I was listening to it. Halfway home, Jeremy pulled his earbuds out and pointed at the radio.

"What's *that?*" he asked. "What are you listening to?"

"Haven't any idea," I said, hitting the OFF/ON button, to bring forth silence.

24

WE ENTER THE BRIGHT HEAT of the kitchen. Jeremy's younger brother, Michael, is usually there, setting the table. (At one time, Laura thought it would be funny if we called Michael "Chad," so that we would have two boys, Chad and Jeremy, in the house, but the joke proved to be too arcane and quickly died.) Our son Michael is a character. He has the intelligent eager expression of a little wolf. Unlike his older brother, who seems straightforward and strong and indulgent, already dad material, Michael is a trickster, a wily pipsqueak shape-shifter. He has a highly developed, but occasionally comic, compassion for the downtrodden.

For this reason he goes through phases. At nine, he threw his lot in with African Americans and claimed himself as one of them. He was enraged when I told him that he couldn't be black, ever, because he himself was white. In his most recent phase, he decided that he was gay (he is now almost twelve) and that we were all to call him "McQueer," which, he said, would be his trademark. At the dinner table his older brother told him wearily that if he went to school demanding that he be called McQueer, he'd get himself beaten up. Michael replied that such a result would be fine. "I can take it," he said, reaching for the serving dish containing mashed potatoes. "Faggots like me have to take it."

"Don't be retarded. And don't call yourself that," Jeremy said.

"What?"

"That word."

"What word?"

"The one you used. Anyway, dummy, you're *not* gay." Jeremy said this through a mouthful of food. "Not this week."

"How do you know?"

"I'm not discussing this. This is ridiculous. Please pass the meatloaf."

"I'm as queer as a three-dollar bill."

"You can't *decide* things like that. Come back when you start dating guys, and we'll talk." Great quantities of meatloaf were shoveled onto Jeremy's plate and quickly disappeared into his mouth. I reminded myself that I should issue instructions to him now and then to chew. But he's getting too old for that. Next year he'll be out of the house. You can't order a seventeen-year-old boy to chew his food.

"Me and my queer friends are gonna do something big," Michael announced. Then he lifted his boyish fist. "Power to the queer nation."

"'My queer friends *and* I,'" Laura corrected him, with a weariness close to Jeremy's.

"Hey, you're queer, too, Mom?" Michael asked, seeing his advantage. "I never knew that."

Changing the subject, my wife inquired, "How was school today?"

"It was a scene of unparalleled horror," Michael told her. "This kid threw up in class."

So much for that. Usually Laura and I let Jeremy be the spokesperson for worldliness when confronted with Michael's latest idea and his latest expression, such as "a scene of unparalleled horror," which, these last few days, he has employed every ten minutes.

"How's German class?"

Michael pointed at the nearly empty serving tray. "Ich muß meine meatloaf haben, bitte."

After going through a phase when he claimed that he would "convert" to African-Americanism, Michael tried to pass himself off as a Communist. "Property is theft," he informed us one night over the tuna-noodle casserole. He was then just barely ten years old. His brother sighed his practiced sigh and asked him if he planned to start a career in shoplifting. Six months later Michael announced that he would grow up to be a Mormon missionary. Mormonism! Where had that come from? Had we heard, he asked us one afternoon, that he would soon leave for Mozambique on a mission? He would have to learn Swahili, or whatever they spoke in that faraway nation, and he would have to do it right away. Jeremy asked him his opinions about Joseph Smith, and Michael said, "Who?" I used to catch Michael reading the encyclopedia—a dangerous hobby with a kid like that. So is surfing the Web. Weird ideas are out there for the picking: he is convinced, for example, that if you turn your TV set to a blank static channel, the dead will find a way to send you a message through the ambient snow on the screen, or through the white noise on the speakers. I have seen him sitting patiently next to the TV set, tuned, he claimed, to the Dead Channel.

Some of his interests, his habits of mind, can probably be credited to me. When he was about six years old, I was dele-gated—Laura ordered me—to go up to his bedroom and tell him a bedtime story. I climbed the stairs and in the dim light began a tale of Heroic Henry. This fellow had been born an orphan in a cabbage field but had been trained by a wizard in bravery, guile, and fighting skills. In the first story, Heroic Henry fights back an army of killer gnomes threatening the village. The villagers reward him with a beautiful house and bride. Then, somewhat abruptly, because I had grown a bit sleepy myself, Heroic Henry dies.

"He dies?" Michael asked, disbelieving, sitting up in bed.

I nodded. Tears threatened to appear on my son's face.

"He *can't* die!" Michael told me.

"Well," I said, "he does. I'm sorry, but that's what happened." I kissed him good night and, after waiting for him to calm down a bit, went back downstairs.

The next night I told another story about Heroic Henry. In this story, he persuades a dragon to eat the lava that is dribbling down from the volcano and threatening the village with incendiary ruin. Then, together, he and the dragon conquer an army of zombie puppets coming in from the West Country. Overcome with thankfulness, the village rewards both the dragon and Heroic Henry with a salary and comfortable shoes. The dragon is put on a retainer. At the end of the story, Heroic Henry dies again.

"This is like last night," Michael told me.

"Sorry. Can't help it. That's how the story ends."

On subsequent nights, Heroic Henry fought off the vollzards—lizard-like vultures—and then he organized picnics and freed various slaves and went to King Alarcord's Mine to retrieve the Biggest Diamond in the World, and he wrote operas and he invented the water-powered automobile engine, and somehow found himself as a relief pitcher in the seventh game of the World Series (he saved the game, of course, for the Toonerville Titans, who had at last made it, after much struggle, into the major leagues), and he rescued the elephants from the evil capitalist poachers who had flown in from Frankfurt, Germany—he is, indeed, a super-hero, but he must meet up with Death at the end. Death, impeccably groomed, is usually wearing a business suit and takes him through the nearest doorway.

After about two months of this, on those nights when Michael was half asleep, he would sometimes tell me to shorten the story. "Make him die," he would mutter.

In January, Michael invited a friend to stay for a sleep-over, and when the boys were ready for bed, he asked me to tell both of them a Heroic Henry story. The friend had a sweet bewildered look underneath a mop of tangled blond hair; his name was Abraham (we were getting into the era of Old Testament names). I didn't think Michael's friend could handle the usual narrative conventions. So I went up there to Michael's bedroom and had Heroic Henry cure King Scotty of the wound in his side, and then Heroic Henry fought off the Yankees, a flock of vampire birds wearing baseball caps, and finally the rains came and saved the village from starvation, and the wheat was harvested, and everyone lived happily ever after.

From his sleeping bag on the floor, little Abraham seemed quite contented. He appeared to be drifting off to sleep.

But Michael was outraged. "He has to die!" he said. "He *always* dies! He's not Heroic Henry if he doesn't die!" I shook my head and turned out the light. Behind me, I heard Michael protesting, "That's not a real Heroic Henry story. That's a fraud!"

"Sorry," I said, behind the closed door. "Tonight he lives."

"No, he doesn't," Michael replied.

He once told me that he knew he had been conceived on

the Moon by Moon People, transported as a Moon Baby on a rocket ship back to Earth, and we, his parents, were trying to foist him off as a normal American boy, whereas in fact he was totally interplanetary.

I agreed with him. Yes, that was exactly what had happened. He expressed dismay with my agreement—he shuffled away angrily. But he's a sweet little lunatic who actually has pretty good sense, and anyway, the sight of him always lifts my heart.

25

AFTER DINNER, the boys disappeared—Jeremy into his room to do his homework, write out his college applications, and call his current girlfriend, Celeste (pronounced "Sell-est"). Like other American teenagers, Jeremy has his own cell phone, and sometimes the two of them simply stay on the phone all evening as they do their homework. I don't see how this is physically possible, but I know that it happens. Jeremy's ear has reddened from having a phone always pressed up against it. He has had one girlfriend or another for as long as I can remember. They adore him—his kindness, his good looks, his gentlemanly manners, and his attentiveness. Even when he breaks up with one of them, he manages to be so gracious that they stick around. It will not be like that once Michael's romantic feelings are stirred up. There will be an air of sickness and apocalypse. Michael will make them crazy.

After Jeremy excused himself from the table, Michael, lacking his best audience, also excused himself—for a wolf cub, he is polite—and, after waving and saying "Tschüss," made a beeline into his own room, the better to read up on his latest enthusiasm, Gay Pride. After half an hour, he would probably get bored with that. A page would turn. *Coca-Cola syrup concentrate is often available behind the counter at drugstores, for certain gastrointestinal ailments*—and few people would know this sly little fact. Michael would be suddenly interested. Coca-Cola syrup! What uses . . . might it be put to?

My wife stood, swept a strand of hair aside from her forehead, and with a laugh said, "Well, it seems we have a gay son." With the back of her hand, she wiped her cheek, a gesture I have always found endearing.

"Could be. But I doubt it."

"Me, too. Well, we're completely unsatisfactory parents for him anyway. In this household, if you came out of the closet to your parents, all you'd get is a bored yawn."

I nodded. "That's it. No closets here. With us, everybody says everything." As she cleared the table, I settled in to add up some receipts, part of our months-long preparations for our income taxes.

Once, about a year ago, in the car as we drove along the back roads to one of Jeremy's swim meets in the next town over, I said to Laura that she and I were like a couple of oxen hitched together, yoked, and that when we had first come out of the stable, no one had known how much work we were good for. As it had turned out, we had accomplished plenty; we were a good team. (We had met when I was still working for Amalgamated Gas and Electric, and she and I had endured periods of tight budgets and some of the terrible economies that can break a marriage.) She was of course offended by my remarks. Oxen? Yoked together? Not a kind analogy. Not very romantic. Her womanly honor was offended.

I'm not stupid. I know that no wife wants to be compared to an ox.

Laura, by the way, is now a collector and dealer in contemporary and classic quilts. I hadn't known about quilting and the system of sales and trading in women's quilts until I met her, but she knows all the networks, African American and white, and she knows all the collectors and the great artists of quilting. She has spent a lifetime learning this trade and learning this art. She loves the work and as an agent takes very little for herself.

In any case, I don't see what is particularly romantic about a married couple raising their children and getting from day to day, and I said so in the car that afternoon. I made my case. The ordinary business of diapers and fevers and broken bones and drafty rooms and lost socks and schedules on the refrigerator door takes the shine off everything for a while. Women understand this better than men do. Why should any marriage with kids be starry-eyed? Romantic heat may start the process off, but dutifulness and pure stubbornness keep it going. Romance—this is my personal view—is a destructive myth after the age of nineteen. Most people give it up, and they should. Percy Bysshe Shelley may have been a great poet, but he had an aversion to raising the children he sired, and he avoided them, and they suffered; you can look it up.

Girls swoon over Jeremy. They can see that he's a practical boy and will be a pragmatic man. Once he's married, he'll be steady. He's a great prospect. Reliability is sexy. Of course, having good looks like his sweetens the whole deal. They attend the swim meets to see him in his Speedo, these girls, avid. They smile to themselves. Their eyes are wide and glistening.

But on that day, Laura was angered by what I had said. She went into a sulk, and even though Jeremy won his event with a personal-best time, she wouldn't speak to me on the trip back home. It was the ox simile, I'm sure.

On the particular evening when Michael had enrolled himself into the Queer Nation, and my wife and I were having one of our ordinary after-dinner clean-ups—me doing the taxes, and Laura, my wife of almost two decades, rinsing the dishes in our suburban home in New Jersey—Laura jerked her head up with a sudden recollection and said, "Oh, by the way. Someone called."

"Who?"

"Someone I never heard of. Said his name was Jerome Coolberg. Who's that, Natie?"

Someone should have complimented me. Only five seconds passed before I said, "Nobody. Well, somebody, from . . . grad school days. Did he leave a number?"

Yes, he did.

26

LAURA AND I have had our own share of shadows. We've been lucky but not that lucky. For years we were poor. I've already mentioned this. When the quilting business was flat, Laura worked as an administrative assistant. I took a second job teaching a night class for immigrants, English as a Second Language. Then there was the accident.

When Jeremy was six years old and Laura was driving him home from day care, she hit a pedestrian who was crossing a street downtown. She had been adjusting the radio to get a better station, and Jeremy had been yelling, and she was distracted. Baby Michael was home with me. This guy was where he shouldn't have been (no intersection and no crosswalk), but Laura didn't see him, and the impact of the car threw him several feet into the air. He went unconscious for an hour or two, had a concussion and multiple fractures, and was in the hospital for over a month. He turned out to be one of those litigious Americans, a real bastard, a pain profiteer. Also an electrician and a drunk, but his alcoholism didn't get into the trial. He sued, of course. It's true that Laura hadn't had her eyes on the road, and it's also true that our Chevy needed brake work. Our insurance was paid up, thank God, but the whole process went on for a couple of years. We were destroyed in some of the ordinary ways, and when it was over, you couldn't find either of us for a while; we had become vague and insulated. I could feel internally the parts of myself that had dried up and withered. Laura said I looked like a tree hit by lightning. I never said to her what she looked like. When lawyers stay calm but keep on talking to you and won't stop, it's as if they're screaming and screaming.

But we're lucky. We got over it. Our next-door neighbors have had the whole menu. Their daughter ran away a couple of times, mismanaged a major cocaine addiction, and was turning tricks in Atlantic City by the age of sixteen. She even had her own pimp. The parents were nice middle-class Americans, churchgoers. They didn't know what was happening to them, or how it had started. Poor American parents: so easily confused. This same daughter got herself enrolled in a recovery program, emerged from it, began cutting herself for fun, then ran away again, this time to San Francisco, where she resumed her career in prostitution. This time she refused help. She accompanied her pimp/boyfriend on a drugstore holdup, was caught and jailed. Her brother, inspired by her behavior, developed a liking for Vicodin. He started stealing prescription pads. He earned his own jail time. Etc. Two kids in the slammer. The father commenced drinking, and why wouldn't he? Catastrophe is contagious. Everyone knows stories like this.

My point is that middle-class life in this country seems to be operating on a contingency basis. It can change on you at any moment. They can pull the rug out from under you. You can be thrown into the street without appeal. Your furniture is carted away; your clothes are tossed on the front lawn;

your children are ground up by a crazy commercial culture. Catastrophe lurks; ruination prospers. As the guy in that movie said, *Ask people for help, watch them fly*.

I went into the den and gazed down at Coolberg's phone number. The numbers in that particular combination had a terrible frightening appearance to me. My hands were shaking, and of course I didn't want to go back there, into that world.

27

ULTIMATELY I WAS REMOVED from Buffalo, but the stages of my breakdown have a montage-like quality to them, and by now they're mixed up with what I have dreamed. My memories of those events were adulterated by the nightly visitations from those people and occasions after the major scenes were over. A sorcerer ruled my imaginings. The music of Mahler served as the background audio sound track. My visitors walked through walls toward me the way Marley's Ghost seeped past the door on his errand to Ebenezer Scrooge. My dreamcallers carried their deadness around with them. Chains clanked. I can't sort out what actually happened from what didn't, and I can't get the dreamstuff out of the narrative. Even though I don't think about that time period often anymore, it accompanies me. My soul was mortgaged. I paid it off through regularity, routine, and hard work, until it was mine again. My history is what it is. Anyway, my crisis occurred decades ago, and I have a life to get on with. So I apologize now for this recon-struction, which is only an outline, a foggy sketchy thing, and for its necessary unreality. Also for its fragmentation. I don't perceive the beauty in brokenness these days, though I once did. But I can acknowledge its truth.

28

I WAS LYING on the floor of my bedroom, praying to God to save Jamie, whom I adored, from all harm. When I came to, someone seemed to have taken away most of my furniture. I was in a blank space unbounded by dimension or time. The apartment had been almost entirely emptied. A mattress remained on the floor, and one book remained, the *Brownstone Eclogues*. No: over there, a book of translations of a German poet, whose name disappears on me every time I read it, sits on the windowsill. The rest of my books had performed a vanishing act. I went to the mirror. Coolberg's face looked back at me. As in a Cocteau film, I fell into the mirror and swam in the glass.

29

SOMEONE IN THE CULINARY ALLIANCE called me, and I drove my VW down to Allentown where the People's Kitchen was burning to the ground. I was surrounded by my friends from the Allentown Artists' & Culinary Alliance. The firemen went about their work with deliberation. Joyous flames shot out from the windows the way they do whenever a particularly effective job of arson has been ordered and set into motion. I was weeping, first, and then violent sobs overtook me. This fire signaled the end of collective generosity in this our country, America. Bent over with sorrow, I was grieving for all our broken promises, for the loss of charity and loving-kindness. Someone reached down for me and ordered me to stand up, someone who looked like Jesus. In the early 1970s, many men in their twenties looked like that. Jesus had broken out on their faces. There was an epidemic of Jesus. What was Jesus doing *here*? I despised him; I had said so. He spoke to me. To this day, I remember that among other instructions, he told me to be a man. Then he vanished into the crowd. Most of his words disappeared from my head almost as soon as he uttered them because Jesus lives solely in the world of dreams. But not the part about being a man. Why did he care about that?

30

THERESA HAS CALLED ME a devil again and apparently I have hit her. Or tried to. She blocked my fist. I might have hurt her. Probably not: she seems *pleased* by my gestural violence. How is this possible? It cannot be possible. She's a feminist. She has been giving me more of her typical knowing smiles. She recognizes that I have been two-timing her and that I do not love her or her irony or her great body. Nevertheless, she continues to ask me for sex, to demand that I fuck her. When I am tender with her, she becomes impatient and angry—that's pretend-love, she says, and from you, it's sickening. We start to get rough with each other in bed. We begin to cross the borders that you shouldn't cross. With her, love is complicated by its opposite, contempt. On the other side of the border is pain and the promise of clarity, but in our case there is no clarity, just more pain.

31

THIS PASSAGE IS a palindrome.

My adored, my beloved. My life. Why did I love her? No explanation is ever satisfactory. How could it be? Jamie had finished her night's rounds, had returned the cab to the central dispatcher, clocked out, and was waiting for the bus in a shelter downtown when she was set upon by a gang. What were they doing out on the streets at that time, five thirty a.m., before dawn? Were they under orders? Why had Coolberg predicted something like this, in *Shadow*? A coincidence, of course, that was all it was, a mere coincidence, a narrative necessity, a required episode of violence against a woman to keep readers awake and alert.

I sat beside her bed in Buffalo General day and night. She would live, they said. A kind nurse named Mary kept us company for several hours, I remember that. Sometimes Jamie would come back to consciousness and look over at me. She whispered from underneath her bandages. *Where was her family?* Where were her girlfriends? Wherever they were, they didn't visit us, though a few of them called, and when I answered the hospital phone, they asked questions, their voices full of concern. But people don't like to visit hospitals, I know, and even an assault can be regarded as infectious. The police questioned her, of course, but her assailants, by striking her, had blurred themselves into nothingness, and she could not detail them. What I finally said was that *I* was her family, and when I did, Jamie whispered to me to take any of the pieces that I wanted, the birds and the dirigibles, from her apartment; she had never made out a will, she confessed. *Am I still alive?* she kept demanding of me, in whispers, as if both the question and the answer were secrets. *It feels like I'm dying.* And I told her she wasn't, and she couldn't; I wouldn't permit it. I saw her pursing her lips, so I kissed her, and she winced.

In the rape, she'd been hollowed out and emptied and smashed up, her broken pieces carelessly glued together in the aftermath, and when she was released, she couldn't bear to be touched or even looked at. She would scream upon being observed. She came to regard her little metallic birds and blimps and tetrahedrons with utter contempt. Junk, trash, leavings, waste. If I wanted them, I could have them all. She hated herself, she hated her work, she especially hated art: sentimental frivolities, all of them, part of a gone world. Life was not like that anymore. Her hatred poured out in a flood, and of course her hatred included me. Because she could not identify her assailants, who had been wearing ski masks, the case remained unsolved, and no suspects were ever arraigned. It took on the phantom existence of something so terrible as to be almost imaginary.

Old women approached me in the street to offer their advice. They flapped their lips silently.

One night Jamie packed up and left her apartment. In a

cloud of unknowing, I let myself in the next morning and discovered that she had moved out. On the table just inside the door she had placed an envelope with a note enclosed addressed to me. I could not open it. I still have it.

My life. My adored. My beloved.

32

"MR. MASON, do you have a view concerning this particular image in the last stanza?"

Yes, I do, yes, actually. Indeed yes. The cold hill's side is a place of spiritual hangover is a place of the pale burning loitering soul is the place of rubble and ash following the fire, the fire that leaves I mean evokes the sweet moan referred to in the hemistich of the concluding line of the stanza, causing the reader to bang his head against the wall, and this is where the knight awakens only to find that he has awakened into yet another dream from which he cannot awaken this time, in a garden of blackened flowers. There has been a rape and an assault, and they have shut her wild wild eyes with kisses four and those dilated eyes have stayed closed.

Everything went dark again, and when I opened my own eyes, from my sprawled position there on the floor of the English department seminar room in Annex B, I saw my fellow students gazing down at me, some with concern, others with curiosity, and I heard a woman saying, "Get help."

33

I WENT INTO that timeless and spaceless realm. Voices circled around me in rooms that were infinitely wide and unfathomably deep. I lived inside the moaning green infinity of my own mirrored existence, where geometrical atrocity reigned, spaces and rooms with boundaries carved out of the air by a diabolical architect. Certain horrors have a strict, dreadful geometry, and I came to know their angles and cosines and tangents. Day and night exchanged their features. Demons favored me. I felt myself sobbing. I lost all desire for the things of this world.

At last, from the chair I sat in, I saw the Hudson River in the distance, and, out of the air of the alcove where I sat, a voice spoke. The voice reverberated from my childhood. I could hardly recognize it. On my windowsill stood a small metallic duck, and from the ceiling hung a little blimp. I found myself in my own bedroom in my parents' apartment on West End Avenue, and when I turned my head, I saw my sister, Catherine, sitting close to me and yet far away. She was dressed in a black turtleneck sweater and a black skirt. The expression on her face was solidly prim, though fierceness lay in it somewhere, and, also, beauty, at a distance. She wore a pair of running shoes.

Her voice emerged from her throat and mouth with a rusty sound like cold water rising up in an antiquated pump. In her hands she held a paperback book. Her general appearance was that of a rather sleek funeral director, but in fact she had clawed her way back to life, and she was dragging me back with her. She had become a force, my sister, on a mission.

Is there anything more restorative than the act of one person reading a beloved book to another person, also beloved? Slowly I returned to my senses.

The rusty unused voice began another narrative. "'About thirty years ago, Miss Maria Ward, of Huntingdon, with only seven thousand pounds, had the good luck to captivate Sir Thomas Bertram, of Mansfield Park, in the county of Northampton, and to be thereby raised to the rank of a baronet's lady, with all the comforts and consequences of an handsome house and large income.'" She took me all the way through *Mansfield Park,* and as she did, the Hudson River acquired a particular color (blue, in sunlight), as did the buildings on this side of it, in Manhattan, and on that side, in Jersey. I noticed people coming and going in my room, and I observed citizens walking to and fro down at ground level, rushing about their business. On stormy days I heard the wind panting against the window glass. In that room, voices became identifiable instead of hallucinatory and generic. Miss Fanny Price eventually disposed of handsome and shallow Henry Crawford and found her match in Edmund. The book ended; my sister started another.

"'In M——,'" my sister intoned, "'an important town in northern Italy, the widowed Marquise of O——, a lady of unblemished reputation and the mother of several well-brought-up children, inserted the following announcement in the newspapers: that she had, without knowledge of the cause, come to find herself in a certain situation; that she would like the father of the child she was expecting to disclose his identity to her; and that she was resolved, out of consideration for her family, to marry him.'" This was "The Marquise of O——," which I'd never read. How had my sister discovered this genius, Heinrich von Kleist? I would have to ask her.

Her readings restored me to life. Gradually I shed the residual toxins of where I had been and what I had done. I moved about in the apartment and prepared my own meals. I toasted bread and put jam on it. I took showers, washed myself, shaved: the little miracles of everyday existence. I tidied up. I avoided reading poetry, and when music came on the radio, I shut it off. Music and poetry both felt disabling to me, part of a world closed and shuttered. Besides, I couldn't bear the stuff in any form. My mother took me down to the shops on Amsterdam Avenue, where I bought new clothes. She left me at the various doors, knowing better than to accompany her adult son into a haberdashery.

From his calm altitudes, my stepfather gazed down at me with mild benevolent confusion. He had adult children of his own from his first marriage. He was under no requirement to love me, his strange irresolute stepchild. So why did he?

34

BUT IT WAS MY SISTER who had become a wonder and a marvel. When the reports of what had happened to me in Buffalo made their way to the Milwaukee halfway house where she lived, she spoke up. Words came from her mouth. She issued a demand: "Take me there." Meaning: to him. To me. My mother flew out on the next nonstop to get her and brought her back to West End Avenue. Catherine—this was reported to me later—saw me sitting in my room, my personhood having been drained out, leaving behind this smeary blotch of nothingness, and, with a cure in mind, she marched over to the bookshelf in the living room. She chose a novel. (I learned later that she happened upon Flaubert's *Sentimental Education*—not where *I* would have started.) I don't remember the thread of the story, though I do remember hearing her voice; for me, the journey was like coming out of an ether dream, accompanied by a woman telling a coming-of-age tale of someone named Frédéric. And somewhere, toward the end of that book, the ether dispersed, or, to use another metaphor, the muddlement in my head began, ever so slightly, to lift, and I saw people and things in the room where I sat, and I heard a story being told to me, and I could tell the difference between the actual things and the imaginary ones.

Later, much later, she told me, "I just wasn't going to let both of us go down the drain."

Her recovery was sometimes referred to as "a miracle," more miraculous than mine, but I don't believe in miracles, just the force of compassion, which under certain circumstances can bring the dead to life. Nor do I believe that to say so is to be a sentimentalist. Though a prejudice exists in our culture against compassion, there being little profit in it, the emotion itself is ineradicable.

After I had come to, I made an effort to talk to Catherine, but she didn't enjoy conversations as much as reading aloud. In fact, she didn't care for conversations at all. Small talk irked her and touched her in the site of her wound. She read to me for another few months, until I was on my feet, whereupon she returned to Milwaukee, eventually found a job, and got herself an apartment. By saving me she saved herself. My stepfather landed me a temp position as a clerk downtown in an East Village sundry shop, where I shelved and restocked shampoos and soaps and condoms. Then I applied for a job at a post office over on Staten Island. I got it. My adult life began. My parents let me go. They released me to the perils and rewards of the world. I moved to another city. I went to work for Amalgamated Gas and Electric, where I met Laura. She had an innocence that moved me. After she gave me a quilt as a token of her love, I married her.

Meanwhile, Catherine thrived, if you can call it that, in Milwaukee, where she resides now. She currently works in a hospice. She plumps pillows and talks softly and reads and actively cares for people she hardly knows. She has never married.

I call her sometimes. I have unanswered questions.

"Why didn't you speak after the accident?"

"I couldn't."

"But when you came home, and you started reading to me, you could."

"That was different."

"How?"

"I don't know," she said. "It just was."

"Because I was in such bad shape?"

"Maybe. I wasn't going to let you go." There was a pause. "Also."

"Also what?"

"You used to call me. Remember? You used to tell me about your life. Stories. Serials." Another pause. "I don't want to talk about this anymore."

"Okay." I had one more question that I had to ask her. "How does the world look to you now?"

"It looks all right."

"You don't think about Dad ever anymore?"

"Sometimes. But, you know, I did all that."

"What was it like, when you weren't speaking?"

"Nate, I have to go."

"All right," I say. "Talk to you next week."

"Right." And then she always says, "Love from here."

And I answer, "Love to you, from us."

35

LAURA SLIPPED INTO the den, where I had retreated clutching the slip of paper with Coolberg's phone number on it. My hand continued to shake. Sometimes the telephone can look like an instrument of studied malevolence.

"Coolberg," she said. "You know, I think I've heard of him. I just can't think of where."

My wife hadn't quite put two and two together. If she had, she would have recognized his name as the host of a program on public radio, *American Evenings*. Although the program's format resembled, in some small respects, other personal-testimony-and-narrative programs on NPR, it had a unique verbal texture and a distinctive angle: Coolberg would begin the program by introducing his guest for that week, a man or a woman with a story to tell—a woman who worked as a writer of inspirational church pamphlets, for example, or perhaps a single father with two children, a man who fixed computers and drove a snowplow in Fairbanks—and although the program would start as an interview, gradually the guest's story would take off, would soar, and at last would reach a moment of disillusion or epiphany that constituted one of those rare moments of clarity, a life-changing instance at first aided by the host's ravening promptings, which gradually diminished and finally disappeared as the show reached its conclusion and the guest found his or her own voice, which was simultaneously the discovery of the story's secret heart. But the show always *began* as a duet between the interviewer and the guest; the guest could not ascend, it seemed, without Coolberg's help in running ahead and lifting the kite of the narrative. Sometimes *American Evenings* sounded like therapy or a church confessional and sometimes like a radio drama in which the tension arose both from the story's conflicts and from the interaction between interviewer and guest. I always found the program funny and enlightening and even moving whenever I could bear to listen to it. My trouble was that I also found the initial parts of the interview peculiar, as if Coolberg sought to make himself invisible week after week by enabling someone else's narrative into existence. He had a hunger, a neediness, to lift someone else up and thus to perform an audio vanishing act for himself, by himself. The story *allowed* him to make a life into art, and then disappear before taking a bow.

One other subtext in the show became apparent every week: as the title, *American Evenings,* intimated, all the stories, all the narrators, somehow pointed toward the phenomenon of disappearances, things and emotions and rituals and forms that had once existed and no longer did, or soon would not. They constituted tales of a twilight as experienced by this culture's citizens. As a result, the show gave off an air of hip nostalgia. People listened to it and wiped away tears while they sipped their martinis or got high.

The format could not have existed without Coolberg, who had an uncanny ability to get under his guests' skins, as if he knew what it was like to be them better than they themselves did. He gave their narratives a structure, understood their gains and losses, and sometimes offered them the key to what they were struggling to say, so that they blossomed into suddenly articulate observers of their own lives, they who had been wordless shadows and subalterns before. He nourished them into a form of *knowing*. He inhabited them by parsing their tales. He squirmed inside their stories and their anonymous selves. Meanwhile, he himself, the unmoved mover, on each of these *American Evenings,* faded, until his voice returned at the very end of the show when he listed the credits for the show's producers, technicians, and corporate sponsors. Underneath his soothing closing words rested a layer of astonishing becalmed rage. You always felt a slight static shock when you heard his voice come on again. You didn't think he could still exist. Where had he gone to? Was his doom always to live inside the stories of others?

"He was a guy I knew," I told Laura. "Back in Buffalo. I've told you about him. He's got that radio show now." I reminded her of it.

After my prompting, she did indeed remember it. He had become quite a personage out there in Los Angeles, by putting his disappearing acts front and center. He had become famously insubstantial.

"Are you going to call him?" she asked me.

"I guess so." I nodded, so that I could agree with myself.

"Your hand is shaking." She reached out and gripped me.

"I'm all right."

"No, you're not."

"Well." I tried to find the right words. "You know: it's hard to find the right words when you're about to talk to someone you once knew when you were someone else, someone you no longer are."

She nodded. The quilt she had given me a few months after we had met each other, her love's token, was up on the wall close to the phone. It had been stitched together, as some quilts are, from rags and cast-off clothes and found fabrics, and the pattern had been set in a series of tiny squares that evoked a child's world of curlicues and stars and snowflakes. What I had always loved about Laura had been her kindness and innocence in the face of the world's sophisticated cruelty. She was almost frighteningly guileless. This meant that about sixty percent of human behavior was simply beyond her comprehension. She had never wised up, and she never would. And yet—I insist on this, too—she was not a child. She just had a permanent immunity to evil. It baffled her.

"All right, I have to call him," I said. "I have to do this myself now. I guess I need to be alone with this."

She nodded and left the room as I dialed the number. "Dialed"! There are no dials on telephones anymore. Nevertheless, the verb lives on in its ghostly phantom way.

A briny-sounding woman answered after two rings, as if from an underwater world. "Mr. Coolberg's office," she gurgled. Background music at her end of the connection could be construed: Bill Evans, one of the solo keyboard albums, where he sounds like a jazz Debussy contemplating which form of addiction he'll try next.

A pause, as I collected myself. "May I speak to . . ." I couldn't say "Jerome," and I couldn't say "Mr. Coolberg," and I couldn't say "Jerome Coolberg," and deciding that I couldn't use any of these terms required an unhealthy and embarrassing amount of time; I was stymied. Finally I said, "Couldn't I speak to him?"

She laughed at the grotesque phrase. "Whom shall I say is calling?"

I gave her my name.

She put me on hold, and a recorded voice came on urging me to contribute to my local NPR affiliate. This was followed by a *blip* on the wire and the sound of something breathing asthmatically into the mouthpiece one full continent away.

"Nathaniel," he said at last.

"Jerome."

"Thank you for calling back."

"You're welcome."

"How are you?"

"Oh, I'm fine, I guess. You?"

He continued to take short stabbing breaths. It was him, all right. "I'm frightened," he said.

"Of what?"

"Of talking to you. This is like swimming across a lake in the middle of the forest and trying to see someone who has been reported as missing, and who may well have drowned. You keep swimming and searching, but you don't want to see what you're supposed to be looking for." Coolberg hadn't lost his taste for epic similes. I had no idea what he was talking about. Sometimes his brilliance just sounded like garble, a form of pre-cognition.

"Uh, right," I said agreeably. It wasn't as if I could *answer* such a statement. "Is that why you called?"

"No."

"Did you want to talk? About—"

"No. Well, yes and no. I've done something. And I need to . . . well, I'm sorry to be so unclear, so vague. I can't really talk about it over the phone. But I need to tell you about it by showing it to you. It's important." Indefinite reference always had a way of proliferating with him, as it did in the fiction of Henry James. After a while, you just lost the thread. Everything turned into "it." At least on the page you could search through the previous paragraphs for what was being alluded to.

"Yes? How? What's this 'something'?"

"I have an idea, Nathaniel. I have an idea of what you should do. A bit of unfinished business that we can finish, you and I. Don't say 'no' until you've heard it."

"Yes? What?"

"If I sent you a round-trip ticket to Los Angeles, would you come out here? For a couple of days? I need to see you in person."

"For what? I don't get it."

"Would you agree to be on *American Evenings*?"

"No."

"That's what I thought you'd say. Yes, that's right. You don't have to agree to it now. I wouldn't expect you to. Think it over. The show can send you tickets anyway, whether you're on the program or not. I could say that I brought you out as a consultant. We have enough in the budget for that. We could put you up in a hotel. You could stay on Sunset Boulevard. It's a well-known hotel we could put you in. Celebrities have died there," he said with a tone of morbid cheer. "The famous Fatal Hotel! Could you come out? Or is the timing inopportune?"

Such talk, thick with unreality, had gone out of my life. I could hear Jeremy upstairs murmuring on his cell phone. No, I couldn't hear him murmuring, not actually, but I could imagine him crooning his love and longings to a girl who would be crooning them back to him. I could see Michael trying to rig up some new use for Coca-Cola concentrated syrup, sold behind the drugstore pharmaceutical counter but not yet properly exploited by the adventuresome early-adolescent set. I could hear my wife talking to a quilter about a purchase on her own cell. "Cell"! That's the word, all right. Everyone else was deeply engaged in his own variety of life. Everyone else inhabited a world. What was I going to do? Spend the rest of my days as a time-server in suburban New Jersey? And never revisit this particular corner of my past, now, in the present, out there in the Golden State?

"No, it isn't," I said. "Okay."

"Okay, you'll come?"

"Okay, Jerome, I'll come."

After arranging where and when we would meet, we said good-bye. How would I manage my absence from the job? I would take two personal days. After I had hung up, I turned to see Laura standing in the doorway, the back of her hand against her forehead, rubbing some irritant away, her eyes fixed on me.

PART THREE

36

THE DAY OF my departure on a very early flight out of Newark, I kissed my wife good-bye as I left the house. She had always been a deep sleeper and barely managed to rouse herself when I leaned down to give her a peck on the forehead. She smiled vaguely at me—at the *idea* of me—and placed her hand briefly on my cheek and then was quickly asleep again, as if she had been visited by a ghost. She muttered, as she always did when she was dropping back into dreams. In Jeremy's bedroom, I saw my older son lost to the world, with his face buried under a blanket, his big feet poking up uncovered at the base of the bed. The room smelled of residual chlorine. After crossing the hallway, I knocked softly at Michael's door. Light streamed out from underneath it.

"Come on in," he said, as if he were expecting me. Did he ever sleep? He was sitting up in bed reading. What would it be this time? *The Anarchist Cookbook?* No: *The Iliad.* You could never tell with Michael. You could never predict the next turn his road would take. On the floor were two CliffsNotes guides, one for the Bible and one for the Koran.

"You should be sleeping," I said quietly, a near-whisper so as not to wake the others across the hall.

"I know," he whispered back. "You should be sleeping, too." He gave me one of his wolf-cub expressions. As a pack animal, he was always happy to see me, the older wolf. "When's your flight?"

"Couple hours from now."

"Dad? When you drink the beverages they give you? Don't ask for ice. Refuse the ice, okay? I read this thing about it. The ice on airplanes has, like, *cesspools* of bacteria in it. The ice'll make you real sick." He scratched his hair and rubbed at his eyes. "And if you can spot any of those Sky Marshals, those FBI guys, let me know. I'd hate that job, sitting on a plane all day, waiting for a terrorist to start the terror show."

"They're not FBI."

"I know. I just said that. It's really TSA. See if you can spot them, though, okay? I bet you can."

"Bye," I said.

"Bye, Dad." I went over to his bed, gave him a brief halfhearted hug (he was at an age when hugs threatened virtually every form of personal stability, but he raised himself up to hug me in return), and was about to go back out when he asked me, "When do you get back home?"

"Day after tomorrow, probably."

"Are you going to be on that radio show?"

"No, I'm not."

He went back to *The Iliad.* "You should get on it. You'd blow them away. You're really good at making stuff up."

I was? That was news to me. I shut the door softly behind me. I walked past the hallway table just beyond the bathroom whose light I had carelessly left on, down the stairs on whose lower landing I inspected a framed picture of a high

school girl whom Jeremy had sketched in art class, out onto
the street where the morning papers were being delivered,
thrown from the passenger-side window of a creeping car. I
greeted the dawn before getting into my car and starting the
engine to drive myself to the airport. I remembered a prayer
I had said years ago on behalf of Jamie, before I had blacked
out. These days, I had lost the ability to pray or to bless.
That gift had abandoned me. It was like throwing words
down into a ditch filled with corpses.

On the airplane, I was seated far back in steerage class, two
rows up from a disabled lavatory smelling of caustic lye.
Before boarding, I had eaten a hasty breakfast in the airport
restaurant, ominously named the Afterburner Lounge. I
was just now beginning to feel the consequences. The food I
had ordered—scrambled eggs that looked concocted from
powder out of a tin—had been served with ill-disguised joc-
ular contempt. The eggs had disagreed with me, so that
when I sat down in my assigned seat, I was almost immediately afflicted. My gut gushed and gubbled.

My seat was next to that of a young mother accompanied
by her squalling son, who appeared to be about a year old.
He clutched a teddy bear with a music box inside. The bear's
head rotated, demonlike, as the music played. Several nearby
seatmates gazed steadily at the teddy bear as if they planned
to dismember it. Meanwhile, the screaming child, in the full
flower of his own hysteria, grew as red as a turnip and as
loud as a megaphone.

The child's mother seemed powerless to stop the sheets
of sound produced by her son. Indeed, she seemed charmed
and surprised by his decibel production.

"Noisy, isn't he?" she laughed. She tried to plug her son's

mouth with a pacifier. He spat it out onto the floor as the plane banked to the left, and the pacifier tumbled out of reach.

"Well, they do scream at that age," I said. This was a lie: Jeremy and Michael had never screamed in this infant-sadistic manner; their cries had always been pointed and specific. The child screamed again, an infant Pavarotti bellowing up to the third balcony.

"Do you have kids?"

"Two sons," I said. "Mostly grown."

The flight attendants pushed the drink carts up the aisle. I kept my attention on the ice cubes. "What did you do with your boys when they were crying?" she asked. "You must have done something. Back then? Men always seem to know about these things. The *fun* things. How did you make them stop?" I assumed she meant the child's outraged cries.

"Oh," I shrugged. "The usual. I dandled them. I bounced them on my knee. I did some peekaboo. I did some bleeump-bleeump."

"What's that?"

"Bleeump-bleeump? Oh, what you do is, you hum the *William Tell* Overture and you bounce them on your knee like they were the Lone Ranger, on Silver."

"Show me?" She lifted up her son and dropped him into my lap. So surprised was this child at finding himself in a stranger's care that his face took on an expression of shock, and he instantly grew silent. I took his hands, positioned him on my knee, and began bouncing him.

To the side, his mother watched this dumb show with admiration. I wondered whether she was pretty. I hadn't really looked at her. I played with her wicked toddler for another few minutes, and when I glanced over at her, I saw that, out of sheer exhaustion, she'd fallen asleep on me.

37

ALTHOUGH MOST AIRPORTS seem to have been de-signed by committees made up of subcommittees, and are inevitably unattractive and unsightly, Los Angeles International has an exuberant ugliness all its own. The atmosphere of non-invitation is quite distinctive, as if the city's first representative, its airport, is already disgusted, perhaps even repelled, by the traveler. The recent arrival might well imagine that he has landed on the set of a low-budget futuristic film, most of whose main characters will die horribly within the first forty minutes. The pods, as they are called, are carelessly maintained, and an odor of perfumed urine wafts here and there through the bleary air.

My fellow passengers trudged out of the plane, blinking like moles exposed to sunshine. The demon-child I had entertained slept, now, in his mother's frontpack. One woman, clearly a tourist, pulled her luggage-slop (beach bag, reticule, cosmetics kit) out of the overhead bin and staggered toward the exit. As soon as she reached the gate, she uttered a disappointed "Huh?" at the ceiling.

It was a common response; several of my fellow passengers sighed with dismay. The airport's unwelcoming skeletal failed postmodernism put most outsiders into a condition of uneasiness. *All this way to the end of the continent, all the trouble we went to, for this?* In every interior nook and cranny, TV sets, hanging like huge spiders from the ceiling, boomed down disinformation from the Airport Channel. You stumble toward your luggage. Downstairs, attendants just past the baggage claim flash expressions of carnivorous appetite at you, estimating the size of your wallet. If you are not a native, the message is, *Welcome to L.A. You're in for it.* If you are a native, the message is, *Ah, one of us. Welcome back.*

Having been to L.A. once on business and once with the family on a vacation, I had armored myself against the ritualistic hostility of LAX. I grabbed my suitcase, made my way past the carnivores to the rental car lot, fumbled with the map, and poked my way out into the hot prettiness of a Los Angeles morning.

Quickly I was drowsy and lost on the freeway, but my disorientation made no difference to anyone. Behind the wheel, I enjoyed a Zen indifference to destinations. Everyone else in L.A. seemed to suffer from a form of permanent distraction anyway, as if, just above the horizon line of their attention, they were all watching a movie in which they played the starring role as they meanwhile meandered about their actual humdrum earthbound lives. Imaginary qualities of actual things predominated here. The spectacular golden sunshine, the hint of salt air and the morning mist rolling in from the Pacific, the occasional views of the hills and mountains upon the lifting of the smog, and the omnipresent aura of dreamy stoned hopefulness—you might as well have been lost on the freeways or caught in traffic, because you were half dead and dazed with it all, the hot petulant loveliness.

What possible goal could you have had that might have been better than where, and who, you were now?

And then there were the cars, alongside of which you could ignore the speed limits or sit waiting for the jams to clear. The captains of industry zoomed past in their pink Bentleys, blue Maseratis, and white Porsches, or in their smoked-glass limos with vanity plates (SILKY was one, DIRECTOR another), and the upper-level drones sported about in their ordinarily luxurious Audis and BMWs. Lower-level types, at the bottom of the food chain, drove the humiliated Fords and humble Chevys, mere shark bait. The street stylists had their lowriders and their bass-driven hubbub. But there was also this museum aspect to L.A. traffic: sitting in a seemingly full-stopped backup, I noticed in front of me a perfectly maintained candy-apple green AMC Gremlin, clown car par excellence, and behind me a blindingly white '64 Ford Mustang. This city, after all, was the North American capital of whimsicality, and if Angele-nos wanted campy remnants from the ridiculous past, they would find them. Here you could spot antique Peugeots and Citroëns and Fiats, Kaisers and Frasers and Morris Minors, Austins and Vauxhalls, rescued from junkyards and given a shine.

The Gremlin, engaged in serious multitasking, talked on his cell phone with his right hand while he electric-shaved his neck hairs with his left. Behind me, the beautiful blond Mustang read the paper and applied lip gloss.

Eventually I found my way to Sunset Boulevard and pro-ceeded toward the Fatal Hotel, where I had arranged to meet Coolberg later in the afternoon. I had always liked the twists and turns of Sunset, its deluxe corridors like roped-off walkways outside of which you might spy distant palazzos whose turrets peeked up above the tactically planted topiary that no drudge was permitted to approach. After living for so long in New Jersey, I simply stared at the palm trees, the bougainvillea, the nature-conservatory greenhouse luxuriance, as I motored past. I didn't want any of it. I just wanted to look, from a safe distance.

When I reached the hotel, a bored valet removed my luggage, gave it to an equally bored bellman, and sped off somewhere in my contemptible rental car. I was ushered into the lobby. For such a famous place, known for its hospitality to louche celebrities of every stripe, the Fatal seemed rather drab, even seedy. It advertised its own cool indifference to everything by means of dim Art Deco lamps and shabby antique rugs. Indifference constituted its most prized form of discretion. To the left of the entryway sat an ice plant. A dusty standing pot with a sunlit cactus in it, close to the elevators, matched the ice plant for pure floral forlornness. They were emblems of four-star neglect. In front of me, and to the right of the front desk, was a brown Art Deco sofa that looked as if it could have used a thorough cleaning. Scandalized, I saw stains. In the sofa's dead center, a model with a high, soft laugh sat talking to a deeply tanned predatory type in a safari outfit who perched on an arm-rest. His teeth gave off a glare of whiteness, and his huge panopticon eyeglasses—an *hommage* to Lew Wasserman—seemed to cover the upper half of his face. He had probably trapped the object of his attention out in the wilds of Malibu and would soon sell her to the slavers. Meanwhile, the half-lit lobby seemed to be recovering from a recent binge. The pale yellow stucco walls radiated the weltschmerz of hangover.

Perhaps, of course, all this feverish registry of impressions was just that—the fever I typically fell into when visiting L.A. I approached the front desk. The clerk sized me up instantly and smiled a shimmering, vacant smile full of patronizing friendliness. He would be polite, dealing with a nonentity such as myself, the smile proclaimed. My banal debaucheries (if I could rise to even that level) would be cosmically inane, however, and laughably conventional. The universe was running down because of people like me. He was already stupendously tired of my existence, and I hadn't yet said a word. On his face was the blasé expression of a young professional who has exactly calibrated which drugs, and in what quantities, are required to get him through the day.

"Yes?" He gave me an affable thousand-mile stare.

"I'm checking in."

The clerk impatiently examined his prizewinning watch. "I'm sorry, sir, but no rooms are ready yet. Check-in time here is three p.m." Well, yes: major-league fun leaves a big mess behind, and didn't I know that? Coolberg would not be meeting me until three.

"Well," I said, "maybe I could check in and turn my luggage over to the bell captain, and take a walk?"

Take a walk! What an idea! Now the clerk actually grinned. An enthusiastic happy disdain flared out of him like the scent of a strong cologne. One did not walk away from this hotel. One was *driven away,* after being loaded into a limo or a hearse. Although he had the random good looks of a would-be actor, the clerk's overbite now protruded slightly when he smiled. Handsomeness gave way to his latent provincialism and failed orthodontics. He would never get more than one line per movie, if that, but what fun I was turning out to be. "Yes," he said. "You *could* take a stroll. Also," he said, remembering his manners, "the hotel has a restaurant. We serve," he said, then paused, unsure of how to finish the sentence, having lost the thread, before catching his thought again, "all day." He licked his upper teeth with his tongue.

"No," I said, "I'll take a walk. By the way, my reservation here was called in, possibly under the name Coolberg. Jerome Coolberg."

"Ah." Sudden recognition; his face brightened slightly, as if a rheostat had been turned to about twenty-five watts. "*American Evenings.*"

"Yes," I lied. "I'm one of them. I'm one of the evenings."

His lips tightened patronizingly, as if at last he had to acknowledge my minuscule somebody-ness. "Congratulations," he said.

Outside the hotel, I walked in what I thought was a westerly direction.

38

ACTUALLY, I KNEW perfectly well where I was going. I ignored the somnolent junkies on the sidewalk and got out of the way of the roller girls zipping past me in the opposite direction. I was intent on my destination. Tempted as I was by the neighborhood record store, still in business and, I could see, patronized by clueless middle-aged men who didn't know how to steal music files from the Web, I nevertheless continued to stride at a soldierly pace, peering in quickly at the tattoo parlors and the magazine racks as I advanced toward the shrine. At last I found it.

Angelyne. There it was, the billboard, dedicated to totally meaningless celebrity. Just as historic literary Long Island had its eyes of Dr. T. J. Eckleburg, so L.A. had Angelyne. She was completely admirable. She had her blowsy showgirl beauty and had peddled it for years in these primary-colored billboards mounted on the roofs of the neighborhood buildings: and in this particularly characteristic one—traditional, just her picture and her name, ANGELYNE—her hazardous giant breasts were on display, though miserably confined by a tight dress of plastic, or was it laminated vinyl? She sported black elbow-length evening gloves, a junk-jewelry bracelet, a cigarette holder, and her aging blond-bombshell hair tumbled on either side of the weather-beaten eyes. Supposedly, according to legend, she drove a chartreuse Corvette. She had once run for mayor.

No one I knew in L.A. had ever paid the slightest attention to these Angelyne billboards. But I loved them. I loved them more than the ocean, more than the Getty Museum, more than the canyons, more than Frank Gehry's Walt Disney Concert Hall. They spoke to the moralist in me. They were like Protestant cautionary tales to the supplicants and votaries of the dreamworld: here, presiding over the beautiful narcotic substances of the city, was this shopworn royalty figure, this majestic ruin, this queen without identity, this ex-beauty, this tautology (her full name was Angeline Angelyne) as powerful in her prodigious way as Ozymandias. She looked out at you, and if you dared, you looked back. You could ignore her; you could pray to her; you could deconstruct her; you could even bother to think about her; but whatever you did, she would continue being as blank and as melancholy as fading beauty itself, brooding down at you from this height, but, like the rest of us commoners, powerless against time.

39

I RETURNED TO the hotel. On the way I bought some postcards and mailed off one to Laura (a picture of the Hollywood sign), another to Jeremy (Malibu volleyball-playing beach bunnies), and a third to Michael (smog). A toothless wizened African American guy approached me and asked me for bus fare. I walked right past him, afraid of a shakedown from a practiced con. Back in the hotel, behind the front desk, the clerk roused himself from his customary insolent ennui and smirked quickly at me before composing himself again. Finding the best seat in the lobby, out of the way of commerce, I sat down to wait until Coolberg arrived. Moths fluttered around inside my stomach. Models and DJs and B-list Eurotrash movie stars came and went.

I felt myself dozing off.

I hate dreams. I hate them when they appear in literature, and I hate them when I myself have them. I distrust the truth-value that Freud assigned to them. Dreams lie as often as they tell the truth. Their imaginary castles, kingdoms, and dungeons are a cast-off collection of broken and obvious metaphors. When you hold them in your hand, you do not hold the key to anything. No door will open. You can live an honorable life without them.

And yet in that lobby, I had a dream in which the two parts of my life were brought together at last. I walked down Sunset Boulevard and entered the People's Kitchen. The place had been restored and spruced up. It was efficient and clean. The dispossessed and hungry who were fed there greeted me happily when I came in. Laura sat near the window and was conversing with Jamie, across from her. They gestured as they spoke. They were both beautiful. The two women leaned toward each other as women friends will, in the great intimacy of shared affections and interests. Jamie had been made whole again. The damage to her had been undone. Here, she was undestroyed. Theresa came by with a water pitcher and poured refills into their glasses. Nearby, my boys conversed with the street people, among whom I saw Ben the Burglar, smiling and laughing, and the old African American man on Sunset to whom I had just refused a handout. Once again I found myself caring for the victims of industrial decline, the poor and ill-fated. My history had been scrolled back and rewritten. I could love anyone and not be punished for it.

40

SOMEONE IN MY DREAM SAID, "Nathaniel, wake up."

When I opened my eyes, I took him in. Standing before me in the hotel lobby was Coolberg, tapping my shoe to rouse me. On his face was the kindest expression I have ever seen on the face of a fellow human. It was angelic, if you could imagine a middle-aged man—balding, slightly overweight, dressed in baggy trousers, rumpled shirt, and unpressed tie stained with spilled food—as angelic. He had the undefended appearance of a middle-aged cherub with a five o'clock shadow and bad posture.

Time had humanized him. I could tell that nothing that he and I were about to do would develop as I had anticipated. The scenario I had foreseen—recriminations, blame, righteous anger—gave way to my sudden intense bewilderment.

"Jerome," I said. I stood and shook his hand.

"Let's get out of this place," he said, glancing around the hotel's lobby with disapproval. "This hotel terrifies me. I thought you might like it. I don't know why I believed that. Out-of-towners are sometimes impressed by it. But of course you wouldn't be." He sighed. "You were never an out-of-towner anywhere," he said cryptically. "I've got a car here and a few errands to run. I drive now. I finally learned how. I learned *directions*. Then maybe we could go out to Santa Monica for dinner. What do you think?"

I nodded halfheartedly. "Seems fine."

His car, a nondescript Toyota, was cluttered with books, DVDs, and plastic pint bottles of chocolate milk, a remedy, he told me, for the chronic sour stomach from which he suffered. He cleared off the passenger-side bucket seat, and within a few minutes we were on Hollywood Boulevard, passing the Walk of Fame. I noticed that Snow White and Darth Vader were circulating there, handling out discount coupons for local businesses. The sunburnt tourists seemed happy to have been given something, anything, by these mythic creatures; they clutched the orange coupons to their hearts. Snow White had been located in that same spot when I had brought my family here on vacation a few years ago. She had had a dotty expression on her face then, and she still had it. The job had deranged her, or perhaps she had suffered from heatstroke and the loss of her worldwide renown.

"Snow White should be institutionalized," I said.

"Oh, she has been," Coolberg knowingly informed me. We drove for another few minutes, and he stopped in front of a supermarket. "I just have to get one thing here," he said. "A seasoning. Want to come in?"

"Oh, I think I'll stay here in the car." I didn't want to find myself following him around.

"Suit yourself," he said.

At the corner, someone with an odd, doughy face was

hawking maps to the stars' houses. Coolberg and I—it was unnerving—hadn't really spoken. He had bragged that the day seemed unusually clear for L.A. (true) and that you could see the hills (also true). Maybe, he said, we should drive up to see "the vista" for ourselves. I had nodded. Sure, whatever. But he hadn't asked me about myself, or my flight, or my past or present life, and I hadn't asked him about *American Evenings,* or his health, or his personal arrangements—whether he was married or partnered or single. We hadn't said a word about the period of antiquity in Buffalo we had shared. Buffalo possessed a drab unsightliness, a thrift-shop cast-off industrialism, compared to L.A., the capital of Technicolor representations. People were leaving there to come here. They were giving up objects for images. Besides, it was as if neither of us had the nerve to start a real conversation.

I looked down at the books in the car. Luminaries: Paul Bowles, Goethe, André Gide, Kawabata, Bessie Head. Books from everywhere, it seemed, many of them old editions with yellowed pages. A notebook was also there on the floor. I picked it up.

The outside of the notebook displayed my name in my own handwriting, Nathaniel Mason, and the date, 1973. I dropped the thing back on the floor as if I'd been slugged. Of course I was meant to see it; I was meant to toss it back onto the floor; I was meant to stare off into the distance, toward the maps of the stars and the brilliantly shabby street, lit by the perky late-afternoon sun.

On our way up one of the canyons—I think it must have been Beachwood, snaking upward just under the Hollywood sign—he kept his silence, but it was one of those silences in which you imagine the conversation that is simultaneously not occurring.

Where are we?

Oh, what a question! We are where we are.

Whose houses are these? Whose castles? What are these hairpin turns?

Don't you admire the camellias? They bloom about this time of year. Those bushes can be pruned into any shape. Note the rose-petal-like flowers, in cream, white, red, or striated colors. Note how they're surrounded by waxy green leaves?

Yes, very nice. We don't have those at home in New Jersey.

What happened to you, Nathaniel? Whatever became of you?

My life changed, that's what. What is my notebook doing on the floor of your car?

Eventually we reached the end of Beachwood Drive, stopped, looked (yes yes, I agreed: an impressive view), turned around, and began to creep back down the canyon on the same hairpin turns. I noticed that he was a rather disordered driver, slow to react, a poor calculator of distance. He was also unobservant, and, I could tell, wearied by the sights. The truth is that L.A. is a company town, and there isn't all that much to show to tourists. Its arid provincial beauty quickly stupefies the innocent and bores the initiate.

"Shall we go to Santa Monica?" he asked, evidently bereft of other ideas. "Should we head out there?"

"Yes," I said. "Let's do that."

41

HE HAD MADE a reservation at a restaurant on Ocean Boulevard, where we had a relatively clear line of sight to the palisade and the Pacific beyond it. It was a coolly perfect late afternoon, with faint wisps of cirrus clouds drifting in from the west. Around us, the cheerful chirps of the local song-birds mixed with slow pensive jazz. A saxophone, played live, from somewhere nearby, curlicued its way through "Satin Doll." From the restaurant's terrace, we were pre-sented with a bright parade of in-line skaters, lovers, and their audiences, and they, too, made me think of tropical birds in brilliant colors, not a crow among them. There was no better place to be. Seated close to us was the usual mix of tourists, domestic and foreign, and local swells, most of them dressed in the gaudy clothes of joy. If you strained to listen, you could hear French and German spoken here and there in the restaurant. No Spanish, though, except back in the serving area and in the kitchen. As a habitué of such scenes, Coolberg took all this prodigality for granted in a way I could not, but he smiled at my keen curiosity, my out-sider's hunger for sights and sounds.

"Would you like some wine?" he asked me. "White or red? Maybe a white to start? They have a wonderful Sancerre here, so they tell me."

"So they tell you?"

"I don't drink," he said, flagging down a waiter and ordering a bottle for me. "I *can't* drink. I go to pieces." The Sancerre came, was poured, was delicious, and Coolberg beamed his kindly cherub smile in my direction as he sipped his mineral water.

"You go to pieces?"

"I lose track of myself."

"Ah," I said, thinking that he had always been guilty of that particular error. I gulped, a bit, at the wine, whose quality was above my station in life. Nevertheless, I was trying to mind my manners. But manners or not, I had business to attend to. "Jerome, how did you find me?"

"Oh, that's easy, these days. You can use the Web to find anybody. There's no place to hide anymore. And if you can't do it yourself, you hire a teenager to do your snooping for you. They know how to find Social Security numbers, credit cards—"

"Yes," I said. "Identity theft."

The phrase hung in the air for a moment.

"But . . . well. Anyway, I had been keeping track of you," he said, going on as if I hadn't said anything. "I knew where you were. Even after I moved out here, to Los Angeles, I studied where you had gone to." He leaned back and glanced out toward the ocean, as if he were contemplating a trip. "You know. What had become of you, things like that.

"It was a little hobby of mine," he continued. "So. When you were engaged to Laura, I found out. That was easy. Really, ridiculously easy. You can't imagine. When you were married, I saw the announcement. That was easy, too—

finding out, I mean. You don't even need a detective for such things. I followed you from job to job, just, you know, keeping tabs, the post office, the gas company, et cetera, all of it from a distance, of course from a distance, *my* distance, where I'd note things down in my record book, and when your son Jeremy was born, I marked the date on my calendar. August twenty-third, wasn't it? Yes. August twenty-third. A good day. I almost sent you a card." He laughed quietly. "And when your wife hit that pedestrian, that vindictive man, I saw the court records of the litigation. Then there was your second son, Michael. A July Fourth baby, born to fireworks, a little patriot, a . . . Yankee Doodle Dandy." He smiled tenderly and tapped his index finger on the table. "I noticed all of the milestones, each and every one of them. My eye was on the sparrow."

I must have stared at him. It was like being in the audience at a show given by a psychic who tells you details about your dead grandmother.

"But why?" I asked him. "Why did you do that? Why did you—"

"Keep track?" He leaned forward. "Please. If you have to ask me such a question, then you're never going to know." I could smell lemongrass on his breath. Probably he drank herbal tea all day. "Your son Jeremy is on the swim team, the breast-stroke and the medley, and your wife has a little business dealing in quilts." He rubbed at his jaw. "Quite a diversified family. I almost bought one from her, and then I thought better of it."

"You thought better of it? You do more than keep track," I said.

"Oh, yes. Sure. I do. I do more. But I won't bore you with additional details about your life. After all, it's your life. You're living it."

It's important to say here that I wasn't angry, or shocked, or disbelieving, or amused by what he was telling me. I was simply and overwhelmingly neutral now, as if witnessing a unique force of nature manifesting itself in front of me. "So," I said, "you became a student of my life."

"Well, obsession stinks of eternity." He reached out for a piece of bread, then spread butter all over it. He hadn't lost his gift for plummy phrases.

"Why *me*?" I had never before seen so much butter applied to a slice of bread. Coolberg had the uncertain etiquette of a child born to poverty, and I remembered that he had always eaten like an orphan in a crowded noisy dining hall. "*Why me*?"

"Why you? You're being obtuse. It doesn't suit you." He glanced to his right as a recently disgraced film actress sat down near us with a female friend. Other people in the restaurant were watching them.

"Well," I said, "as long as we're talking about this, do you know what happened to Theresa?"

"Theresa?" he laughed. "Her? Oh, she scuzzied herself back into the great membrane."

"What does that mean?" Twilight was beginning to come on. The waiter lit the candle on our table. The ocean currents went their way. Planet Earth hurtled through space. The galaxy turned on its axis.

"She wasn't much to begin with, was she? And she wasn't much later either. So now, I imagine, she isn't much at all. All that tiresome irony of hers, that sophomoric knowingness. I don't think irony as a stance is very intelligent, do you? Well, I mean it has the appearance of intelligence, but that's all it has. It goes down this far"—he held his hand at knee level—"but it doesn't go any farther."

"She was pretty," I said, feeling the need to defend her.

"No," Coolberg said. "I don't agree. Theresa was attractive without being pretty. She had the banal sensibilities of a local librarian who's moved to the big city and has started serious drinking and making semi-comical overstatements to disguise her obvious gaps. All those Soviet medals! Come *on*. And one memorized line of French poetry. What a doofus she was. Poor thing. There's a difference between—well, attraction and prettiness, and she never got it. All of her books were borrowed, if you know what I mean. Anyway, she's wherever she is."

"But you were her lover."

He blew air out of his mouth in response to this irrelevant observation.

"And Jamie?" I asked quickly. "Jamie Esterson? The sculptor? She worked at the People's Kitchen, remember?" I felt a shadow fall over me, as if I were about to get sick very soon. Could you become mentally destabilized in an instant? People talk about panic attacks, the feeling of the sudden oncoming locomotive and you, caught on the tracks in a stalled automobile. Anyway, I saw the shadow there, and I fought it off by looking out at the sidewalk and quietly counting the cars on Ocean Boulevard. Fourteen, fifteen, sixteen.

He flinched. "I don't know," he said. "I don't know what happened to her. No idea at all."

Eighteen, nineteen, twenty.

He ordered the salmon, and I ordered the cassoulet. Night dropped its black lace around us. He began to tell me what had happened to him. After leaving the East and never quite collecting a college degree, he had turned up in Los Angeles, having written a screenplay, a musical, *Fire Escape,* whose odd

locale had been a downtown apartment building with a cast
of colorful urban characters ("If you could imagine *Rear Window*
as a musical, which I could, in those days, then you could
imagine the script"). Although the screenplay had been
optioned, the project went nowhere, but its readers noticed
a certain flare in it, a soigné knowingness about plot require-
ments and genre conventions. Slowly he built up a lattice-
work of friends, among them a programming manager at a
local public-radio affiliate. Oh, this was dull. He would not
bore me any longer with the banal details of what he had
accomplished and where he had been and whom he had
known. He had a life. Everyone has a life. If I cared, I could
check on it. I could hire my own gumshoe teenager to snoop.
No one cares about the particulars, he said—an obvious lie
and the first mis-statement to emerge from his cherubic
face so far. He was, after all, the host of *American Evenings.* In a
sense, he was hosting it now. This was one of those evenings
he so prized.

"I'm interested in the particulars," I said, tipping back my
third glass of wine. The waiter came to pour the remainder
of the bottle's contents into my glass. "Such as: Are you married?" I thought of current conversational protocols. "Do
you have a partner? Is there someone?"

"Oh, there's always someone," he said vaguely, dismis-
sively. He watched an old man rumble by on the sidewalk
stabilized by a walker. He was accompanied by his elderly
wife, and both were wearing identical blue blazers. No: they
were not married. They were twins.

"Who's yours? You seem to know about mine," I said.

"What does it matter? Are you trying to take a moral
inventory? It wouldn't be anyone you know. Love is generic.
Besides, that's not what you're really interested in."

"What am I really interested in? Since you seem to be the expert."

"Well, okay, to start with, here's a subject of interest: What am I doing with your notebook from years ago? Why was it reposing on the floor of my car? Which you surely took note of, that notebook, when I was in the supermarket buying garlic and arrowroot?"

"I did."

"Isn't it interesting?" he asked. "So far, we haven't talked about those days. You never asked me back then, or ever, why I had your clothes stolen or why I was wearing them. You went around with that expression on your face as if you understood each and every one of my actions, as if you understood everything and accepted all of it. No one will ever tell you this except me, so I'll say it: that expression appeared to comprehend *everything* that anybody could present to it. Your tolerance was positively *grotesque* in its limitlessness. What *didn't* you accept? It was your greatest weapon. No: your second-greatest weapon."

"What was the first?"

"Want another bottle of wine?"

"I've had enough."

"So what? Who cares? You're not driving anywhere." He made a gesture at the waiter, and instead of wine ordered brandy. Then he began teasing his lower lip with his index finger. "Why do you care about that sculptor so much, that Jamie person? Why *did* you care?"

I reached for my wineglass. "Because I loved her. Because I never got over her."

"Are you sure about that?"

"Yes. About that I am very sure." My syntax had acquired the stately formality of the truly inebriated. I was still wondering what he thought my greatest weapon was. "And by the way, who are you to be interrogating me about any of this?"

He smiled an impish smile. "The host of *American Evenings,* that's who. And look. That's exactly what we've been presented with." He pointed in the general direction of the Pacific Ocean. "A pleasantly wonderful American evening for the consumers of twilight and our national metaphysical ruin, as played out here, in the best of all possible worlds, in SoCal."

I wasn't sure that I had heard him correctly. "'SoCal'?" Had he really employed that usage? "So this is another one of your *American Evenings*? You don't have your tape recorder on, do you?"

"Oh, no, Nathaniel, that would be illegal, immoral, and, what's worse, impractical. You can't pick up an adequate—"

"What did you do to her?" I interrupted him.

"To whom?"

"To Jamie."

"To Jamie? *I* didn't do anything to her." He leaned back. "She was set upon. By dogs."

"But you predicted it. You told me that day in the zoo. You said you were writing something called *Shadow,* whose story contained an Iago-like character named Trautwein, I remember that, who is tormenting another character, I think his name—and it was truly a ridiculous name, an affectedly literary name—was Ambrose, who loves this woman, an artist, and Ambrose . . . well, the person he loves is harmed, not directly, but by hired-out third parties. It's not *Othello,* but it's a third cousin once removed to that story. Trautwein sees to the harm." I winced at my own alcoholic repetitions, but they were essential to the case I was making.

Somehow, coffee had appeared on the table. Coolberg picked up his cup. "It might have been a coincidence."

"Okay," I replied to him. "But what if it wasn't? What if . . . let's just say . . . *hypothetically* . . . what if you, or, um, someone *like* you, not you exactly, not you as you are now, what if this hypothetical past-tense person had hired . . . what if you had hired some young men, some thugs, for example, that you found hanging around the People's Kitchen or some place like that, to beat her up, to do terrible violence to her? Well, no. Strike that. I take that back. Maybe all they were supposed to do was threaten her a little. A teeny-weeny act of intimidation, motivated by jealousy, let's say. That's all. They would walk up to her at the bus stop and slyly put the fear into her. And this . . . prank would scare her right out of town. Off she would go, to another . . . what? Venue. That was the goal. You know: give her a little 12-volt shock. Affright her with their boyish street-thug menace, which is, I might add, celebrated now on all the major screen media. We can't get enough of *that,* can we? Sweet, sweet violence. So, anyway, with this plan, she'd leave town, pack up herself along with her few minor bruises, if she had any, and move, taking her little birds and blimps with her. But maybe the plan goes awry. Let's suppose that the guys who are hired are not just sly. They're criminal sociopaths instead. The 12-volt shock turns out to be 120 volts. And then it gets European and goes up to 240 volts. And what if . . . let's just say . . . they got into it, these thugs that'd been hired, or were maybe just doing a favor—well, you'd only need a couple of them, and they couldn't stop what they had started, their specialty not being staying within limits set for them by authority figures, after all, and they hate women anyway, and they sort of raped her, because it was possible, you know how one thing leads to another, don't you, Jerome? I know I do. And she *was* raped. And after it happened, she couldn't remember much of anything, so there were no arrests and no trials because she couldn't identify anybody and the police were helpless, and she left town soon afterward, clearing the field, so to speak. What if *that* had happened?"

He looked directly at me. "Then I would have been a monster." He glanced at the sky. "Then I would have been unable to live with myself."

"But you had already hired a burglar. You had hired a burglar to steal clothes, *my* clothes, and then he got into his tasks, and he couldn't stop, and he stole everything from my apartment, until nothing was left, only a book or two. And a mattress." I leaned back. I felt like repeating myself. "You *had* already hired a burglar. It's what you do. You're still a burglar. You still steal clothes. I've listened to your show."

"Is that what you think happened?" he asked me. "Is that really what you think?"

"Sometimes I think it," I said. We were both speaking calmly, like gentlemen, over the coffee and the dessert.

"You think your apartment was being emptied by burglars?"

"Sure it was."

"Oh, you poor guy," he said. "It wasn't being emptied by *burglars.* It was being emptied by you. You were moving out, or trying to. Don't be such an innocent. You were trying to move in with her. With that Jamie person. This hopeless hopeless stupid idiotic romance you thought you had going on with her. It was making you crazy, you poor guy. We could all see it. Anybody who loved you could see it. And of course she wouldn't let you take anything over there, into her place. Because there was no room, to start with. And because she didn't love you the way you loved her and . . . she didn't really want you over there. So you were storing your stuff somewhere else, in the meantime, until she would *come around,* as we used to say, come around to being the benign woman you believed she could be, the heterosexual wife or whatever she was that you had envisioned. You had assigned a certain set of emotions to her and were just waiting for her to have them, and meanwhile you were reading that soggy Romantic poetry and dragging the spectacle of your broken heart across the Niagara Frontier. Love? You were offering something you didn't have to someone who didn't want it."

"I was storing my stuff somewhere else?"

"Of course you were."

"If she was refusing me, why wasn't I taking my stuff back to my own place?"

"Because that would have been an admission of defeat. You were always good at denial."

"So where was I taking everything?"

He gave me that look again. "You poor guy," he said again. "You persist in your habits, don't you? Your ingrained habits of incomprehension. *Willful* incomprehension. And convenient amnesia. You're just like this country. You're a champion of strategic forgetting. You really can't give up your innocence, can you? That sort of surprises me." He glanced down at my glass of brandy as if it were responsible for my faults. "You can't live without your disavowals. You told me that Jamie left you a letter behind in her apartment after she took off. It was addressed to you."

"Yes."

"What did it say?"

"I never opened it," I admitted.

"I rest my case," Coolberg said, signaling for the check. "Let's go down to the pier."

42

I SUPPOSE HE MUST HAVE loved me back then. He must have enjoyed being me for a while, wearing my clothes and my autobiography. And I suppose I must have noticed it, but I never thought of his emotions as particularly consequential to anyone, and certainly not to me—the feelings being unreciprocated—and in those days, brush fires of frustrated eros burned nearly everywhere. Everyone suffered, everyone. I myself burned from them, and when you are burning, you are blinded to the other fires.

Next I knew, we were out on the Santa Monica pier, making our way toward the Ferris wheel, as if we had a rendezvous with it. After the wine and the brandy, I thought the structure had a giant festive beauty, with exuberant red and blue spokes aimed in toward the white burning center. Ezekiel's wheel, I thought, a space saucer of solar fires. Give me more wine. My emotions had no logic anymore, having been released from linearity, and certainly no relation to the conversation we had just had, Coolberg and I. Multicolored plastic seating devices that looked like toadstools affixed to the Ferris wheel lifted up the passengers until they were suspended above the dull sea-level crowd. Coolberg was speaking; I could register, distantly, as if from my own spaceship, that he was uttering sentences, though their meaning appeared to be comically insubstantial. Slowly the words came into focus. He noted that during the day, the wheel on which we were about to ride was solar-powered, could I imagine that? A solar-powered Ferris wheel! Just as I thought! Energy from the sun lifted this thing. Only in L.A. He bought two tickets. From somewhere he had obtained a bag of popcorn. All around us we now heard Spanish spoken by the eager celebrants, the Ferris wheel being a bit too unsophisticated for your typical pale-faced tourist out on the Santa Monica Pier. This ride was more suited to the illegal immigrant population that understood distance, death, and sweep.

"Mira. Hoy, los latinos," Coolberg whispered to me. "Mañana, los blanquitos."

We were ushered onto one of the blue toadstools with an umbrella canopy obligingly suspended over it, and before I could register my objections, Coolberg and I were locked in, a gesture was made, and the wheel scooped us up into the air.

We went up and down, he and I.

"It would be nice to say that I'm asking for your forgiveness," he was saying, somewhere nearby me, as we swayed in the air, and swooped, "but I've tried to eradicate sentimentality from my daily routines, and besides, you're too drunk. You're not going to remember any of this, and forgiveness induced by alcohol, from you, is meaningless. What I really want to do is explain something to you."

The wheel lifted us up again, and I saw Malibu ahead of us, and Venice Beach behind (the toadstools twisted on some sort of pivot), diminish into starfields, in the way that a city, seen at night from an airplane whose cabin has been dimmed, will look, with its spackled pinpoints, like the sky that mirrors it. Directly below us the carnival sounds of the Santa Monica Pier faded into an audible haze, and I could feel my stomach lurch.

"I have admitted nothing," he said, "and I have confessed to nothing. I haven't asked for your forgiveness, because forgiveness has a statute of limitations attached to it. If it comes too late, the emotion itself has expired. *Pffffft.* It only works if it's fresh, forgiveness; and when it's stale, it's rotten and useless. Don't you agree? But, you know, I was sorry—really I was, horribly sorry, disgusted, mortified, disfigured with regret, oh, just fill in all the adjectives you want to. I'm sure you can do that. What was I saying? I remember. I was sorry about what happened to that girl, that Jamie, your one true love, and if those days could have been taken back, if I could go back there, then I would certainly have taken that journey and *taken* them back. If I could have gathered all those people in my arms—you and Theresa and Jamie and your sister and your father and all those other people we knew and didn't know and didn't even care about—and carry them away to safety, I would have, believe me. And then I'd save the Armenians from the Turks, and the Jews from the Germans and the Poles, and the Tutsis from the Hutus and the Hutus from the Tutsis, and the Native Americans from us, as time is my witness, I'd do that, but, hey, come on, *who are we kidding?* That's marauding sentimentality, there. There's no protecting anyone once history starts digging in its claws, once real evil has a handhold, and besides, what I did . . . well, look down. Are you looking down? Nathaniel? Good. Do you suffer from vertigo? I do. But you see what's down there? I don't mean the ocean. I don't mean the salt water. Nothing but idiotic marine life in there. Nothing but the whales and the Portuguese and the penguins. No, I mean the mainland. Everywhere down there, someone, believe me, is clothing himself in the robes of another. Someone is adopting someone else's personality, to his own advantage. Right? Absolutely right. Of this one truth I am absolutely certain. Somebody's working out a copycat strategy even now. Identity theft? Please. We're all copycats. Aren't we? Of course we are. How do you learn to do any little task? You copy. You model. So I didn't do anything all that unusual, *if* I did it. But suppose I did, let's suppose I managed a little con. So what? So I could be you for a while? And was that so bad? Aside from the collateral damage? Anyway, I may have bought something, *but I never paid for a rape.*"

He stared off toward the darkness, and the lights, of Malibu.

"Let the British be the British," he said, out of nowhere. I was losing the thread. "We know what they're like, the Brits: stiff upper lip, a nation of shopkeepers, sheepherders, whatever, all the same, the Brits. We know them. But no one knows who we are here, in this country, because we're all actors, we've got the most fluid cards of identity in the world, we've got disguises on top of disguises, we're the best on earth at what we do, which is illusion. We're all pretenders. Even Tocqueville noticed that. And if I was acting, anyway and after all, so what? *I was just being a good American.*"

"Stop talking," I said. "Shhhhh. Don't say another word."

"No?"

I held my finger to my lips. "Shhh."

The wheel turned in a temporary silence.

"That was a very good speech," I said. "You were always good at imitating eloquence."

"Thank you."

"But I know what this is," I said. "This is an imitation, isn't it? All planned out. This is an imitation of Joseph Cotten and Orson Welles in that movie, *The Third Man.* How clever you are, Jerome, how devious," I slurred. "Italy, the Borgias and the Renaissance, Switzerland, a thousand years of peace, and cuckoo clocks, Harry Lime's big speech justifying himself. Everything becomes a reference, to you, doesn't it? You're so *knowing.* What *don't* you know? Everything evokes something else, with you. Just as you say."

His eyes appeared to be wet, but he smiled proudly. I had found him out. He was still pleased to be my friend. He could cry and be pleased with himself at the same time.

"You said you had something to show me," I told him. "Where is it?"

"I wasn't sure you'd remember."

"Oh, I remember," I said. "You told me over the phone that you had something, and you were going to . . . give it to me. Where is it?" I waited. "It's not that old notebook of mine, is it? Because if that's what it is, I don't want it back. Or anything else I gave to you, all those years ago, for storage."

He leaned over. His popcorn spilled out onto the floor. I think he was about to kiss me on the forehead. I leaned back, and he made a gestural lunge. The Ferris wheel's toadstool swung back and forth.

"None of that," I said. "Too late now."

"Oh, okay," he said.

"So where's this thing you have for me?" I asked again.

43

THE WALK BACK to his car seemed to prolong itself almost into infinity, as some experiences do on the wrong side of marijuana or alcohol. Some distortion or injury had occurred to my sense of time, and I could not get back into the easy clocklike passing of one moment into another. All he had told me was that the gift he had for me, whatever it might be, was back in his apartment. I think I died on the way to that car.

Somehow—it seemed to be many years later—we arrived at his Toyota. He unlocked it. I sat down on the passenger side.

44

AFTER A DRIVE whose duration in time I could not have estimated in either minutes or days, we entered, he and I, the infested interior of his apartment. The curtains, thick with grease, had turned from white to gray. Just inside the door, a three-legged cat hobbled over toward him and propped itself against his leg while the two of us examined the newspapers, magazines, books, and framed pictures scattered on the floor, the bookshelves and kitchenette table, and the sofa cushions. Elsewhere, VHS tapes and DVDs had been piled up along the wall, arranged by genre and alphabetized. Outside the window, the lights from passing cars swerved dimly in and out of view, leaving shadows on the ceiling. A calendar near the doorway had been thumbtacked to the wall and showed the month of December from three years ago; the accompanying picture, in faded colors, was that of a sleigh followed distantly by wolves. Through the doorway facing me, a kitchen sink was visible, illuminated by a 1950s-style overhead fixture; the sink's faucet dripped softly and steadily, leaving a slime trail of rust. Green wallpaper adorned the kitchen. A silenced German clock hung at eye level; the time, it claimed, was nine fifteen. In a corner a TV set had been left on, though the sound had been muted. On the screen, a gigantic blue monster—the TV's picture tube needed to be replaced—with fish-like scales and a long ropy tongue ripped its claws silently into human flesh. Blood spurted terribly against a suburban home; children ran screaming away. No doubt people were shouting, and frightening music would have been blaring on the sound track if only the volume had been turned up. Over in another corner, a radio, tuned to an FM classical station, played one of the piano pieces Schumann had written late in his madness when he claimed the angels were singing to him.

The masses of accumulation were piled so thickly in the living room that paths had been made between them to allow passage toward the bedroom and bathroom.

As an apartment, this one was not so unusual, especially for a single man. Cluttered and disorderly, every item indisposable, the spaces filled with the wrack and ruin of a solitary life, this apartment served up an antidote to emptiness with a messy mind-stultifying profusion. The rooms looked like the temporary unsupervised housing of someone with a ravening spiritual hunger, a grandiloquent vacancy that would consume anything to fill up the interior space where a soul should be. Books were piled and stacked everywhere. Behind this craving resided an urge as strong as love. All the furniture was secondhand, scratched—emergency furniture to be used in case a catastrophe occurred, as indeed it had. The dreadful had already happened. The catastrophe had come to pass and would last for a lifetime.

The cat purred, and the monster on the TV set was now attacking a major U.S. metropolis. These rooms were filled up but still empty, as empty as the vacuum of outer space uninhabited by a living being, and yet the place had retained its ability to project a human solitude and loneliness, as did Coolberg, who gazed at his dominion with a resigned expression of deadened appetite.

The clotted and crowded emptiness was so thick that it was almost impossible for me to breathe. The clutter seemed to be using up all the oxygen, as if it were inhaling itself. Coolberg placed a small spice bottle of powdered garlic, and another of arrowroot, on the stained kitchen counter with a slightly theatricalized pathos. Then he looked at me. His expression seemed to be one of ecstatically sorrowful triumph. He reached for something on the counter, couldn't grasp what he wanted—a box of some sort—so he took a step into the kitchen, scooped up what he had tried to pick up, and brought it back.

"Here," he said shyly.

I lifted the lid. It was a typed book manuscript. It was entitled *The Soul Thief*.

"I wrote your story for you," he said. It began, "He was insufferable, one of those boy geniuses, all nerve and brain."

Reader, what you hold in your hands is the book he wrote.

45

YOU WILL SAY, this is a trick. You will say, "This is the last twist of the knife that eviscerates the patient." But a disagreement is offered: this narrative turn contained no trick; it comprised the story itself. And didn't the details leave you every possible clue? On every page the narrative intentions were plain, even obvious, starting with the reference to *Psycho* and going on from there. He played by the rules. He played fair.

But the point cannot be that one person can take on another's life, and in identifying with the other, give life to himself. Such a modest observation! We all know that. The point must lie elsewhere.

The point is that although love may die, what is said on its behalf cannot be consumed by the passage of time, and forgiveness is everything.

PART FOUR

46

Nathaniel Mason enters the silent house. I can easily imagine it. He drops his suitcase softly on the foyer floor. "Hello?" he calls out. No one returns his greeting, except for the floorboards beneath his feet, creaking happily, pleased to be weighted down. He can see through the door to the kitchen, and, through the kitchen, to the backyard beyond. A dour, cloudy day. Behind him is a shadow. From now on, the shadow will always go with him. The mantel clock, knowing its one set of facts, smugly chimes on the quarter hour for him. Midafternoon: his son Jeremy will be starting his swim practice any minute now, and his son Michael is . . . well, who knows where Michael is? Michael investigates, in his own way, the multifarious mysteries of the world. And Laura? She is not here, either, it seems, but he calls out to her anyway. "Laura? Honey? I'm home." The silence of an empty house returns to him. The furnace ignites with a subterranean whoosh and chuckle. Laura has followed the daily schedule and is, even now, watching out for the boys, or she stands in a room, checking with her expert eye the textures of a quilt.

He will tell Michael that, on his advice, he did not accept the bacteria-infested ice cubes on the airplane's refreshment cart. He will tell Jeremy that Snow White and Darth Vader still ply their trade on Hollywood Boulevard. He will tell his wife that he discussed being on *American Evenings* but then thought better of it. He will kiss her as she enters the house.

He will not quite say that he has given up everything for this settled domestic life, the one that he cherishes and loves. He will not quite say that his public life is, in its way, a secret inside a secret. That he, in his way, is also a soul thief, and that the soul he has stolen belongs to a lesbian ex-sculptor who lives somewhere far away, and, in all probability, alone. And that he now lives, and will go to his grave, accompanied by another.

Nathaniel has the house to himself. It is his, in temporary solitude, except for his shadow. He ascends the stairway. He pushes aside the door to Jeremy's room.

Nathaniel Mason approaches the desk cluttered with Jeremy's litter. Right there, on the left-hand side of the desk, is the draft of an essay for a college admissions form, printed out from Jeremy's computer. Nathaniel bends down to read it.

The Things We Take for Granted
BY JEREMY MASON

What do we take for granted? And is taking things for granted natural, or a mistake? Or somehow both? When I ride the bus from my home to Emerson High School, which I attend, I know where all the curves in the road are way ahead of time. I can anticipate traffic jams. My fellow students sit in the same seats most days. I even know where there will be dogs barking in the neighborhood. Believe it or not, I know the names of some of the dogs because I have walked them, as a summer job! Thank goodness we, as humans, are capable of anticipating some events! That way, we are able to make plans. We can save money for a rainy day. We can outline a strategy, a plan of action. Otherwise we would be in the dark all the time, experiencing surprises each and every minute. Surprises are good but not when they are eternal. But there are some things that we must not ever take for granted, three above all. We should not take for granted our families, our beliefs, and our [strengths and weaknesses? loved ones? health?]

No one should ever take his or her family for granted. For example, my younger brother is weird, but he is always surprising me by how fearless he is. Last week he said to the family that he is planning to travel to India alone this coming summer to be "enlightened" by a guru he found on the Web, which I know for a fact he is not. He likes to attract attention to himself but he is basically harmless and courageous. He has said he is gay, but that was grandstanding. For example, I have seen him staring long and hard at *Playboy* magazine. My mother is quiet but she is always there for me and is always rooting for me in my athletic endeavors and academic achievements and is always in my corner. She keeps on me to study carefully and to give everything I can to academics and athletics. My dad too is quiet, but just as the old saying is that still waters run deep, I know that he

Nathaniel turns away from the page. In its cage to the side of the desk, Jeremy's pet white rat, Amos, sticks its nose out from its bedding to see if anything is going on. Outside, a car may be pulling up in the driveway. Whatever his son has written about him can wait for his inspection. Soon they will all be home, his wife and his two children, and Nathaniel will have prepared a salad, peeled the potatoes and boiled them for mashing, and he will have laid the steaks tenderly on the grill. Will green beans be served? That depends. The front and back doors will rattle open, and tumult will fill the house as it does every evening. Laura has left him a note informing him where the dishes are hidden away in the refrigerator, and how he should prepare them. "Welcome home, sweetie," the note begins, and it continues, "Were you on the radio? If you're clueless about the dinner dishes, you should start by . . ."

(In the basement, near his worktable, where he is assembling a small blue birdhouse to be hung on the apple tree in the backyard, stands a compact companionable metallic duck, sturdily upright on its two metal legs. In the drawer of his worktable rests a sealed envelope. And inside the envelope is a folded message, surely a benediction, he believes— this hope constitutes his last article of faith, which he will clutch until the end of his days.)

Blessings, he thinks, on my family, on the poor and helpless, the brokenhearted, on the victims of violence and on its perpetrators. May they all be undestroyed. Blessings on everybody. Blessings without limit.

A last visit from Gertrude Stein, as she waves good-bye: *For a long time, she too had been one being living.*

Minutes later, in the kitchen, he takes the dishes out from the refrigerator one by one. He begins the preparations for dinner.

NOTES

This is a work of fictions.

In this novel about thievery, I am happy to acknowledge some borrowed gifts. Theresa is correct about Coolberg's dream: it does not belong to him but to Diane Arbus and can be found in her 1959 notebook #1, as printed in *Revelations*. Coolberg also has a habit of quoting, without attribution, passages from Joseph Stefano's script for *Psycho*, along with other passages from the novels of E. M. Forster. The quotations from Gertrude Stein are largely paraphrases of her portrait of Matisse. The translation into English of Kleist's *The Marquise of O——* is by David Luke and Nigel Reeves.

For certain details about Los Angeles flora and fauna I am grateful to Francesca Delbanco and Arden Reed. My grateful thanks also to Michael Collier and Louise Glück. The story of Simple Shmerel is derived from *The Adventures of Simple Shmerel* as told by Solomon Simon. My thanks to Carl Dennis for bringing these stories to my attention.

As always, thanks to Liz Darhansoff, Carol Houck Smith, Dan Frank, and Martha and Daniel Baxter.

ABOUT THE AUTHOR

Charles Baxter is the author of eight other works of fiction, including *Believers, Harmony of the World,* and *Through the Safety Net. The Feast of Love* was a finalist for the National Book Award. He teaches at the University of Minnesota.

A NOTE ON THE TYPE

The text of this book was set in Requiem, a typeface designed by Jonathan Hoefler (born 1970) and released in the late 1990s by the Hoefler Type Foundry. It was derived from a set of inscriptional capitals appearing in Ludovico Vicentino degli Arrighi's 1523 writing manual, *Il Modo de Temperare le Penne.*

Composed by Stratford Publishing Services,
Brattleboro, Vermont
Printed and bound by R. R. Donnelley,
Harrisonburg, Virginia
Designed by Wesley Gott

12/09
3/0
6/08